TRIAL BY LEVIATHAN

OPERATION MARRAKESH
BOOK 1

BLAZE WARD

KNOTTED ROAD PRESS

Trial by Leviathan
Operation Marrakesh, Book 1
Blaze Ward
Copyright © 2024 Blaze Ward
All rights reserved
Published by Knotted Road Press
www.KnottedRoadPress.com

ISBN: 978-1-64470-396-0

Cover art:
ID 126123651 © Freestyleimages | Dreamstime.com

Cover and interior design copyright © 2024 Knotted Road Press

Reviews
It's true. Reviews help. Even a short one, such as, "Loved it!" So please consider reviewing this book (and all of the ones you've read) on your favorite retailer site.

Never miss a release!
If you'd like to be notified of new releases, sign up for my newsletter.

http://www.blazeward.com/newsletter/

Buy More!
Did you know that you can buy directly from the Knotted Road Press website?

https://www.knottedroadpress.com/shop/

ALSO BY BLAZE WARD

The Jessica Keller Chronicles

Auberon

Queen of the Pirates

Last of the Immortals

Goddess of War

Flight of the Blackbird

The Red Admiral

St. Legier

Winterhome

Petron

CS-405

Queen Anne's Revenge

Packmule

Persephone

First Centurion Kosnett

Encounter at Vilahana

Consensus at Aditi

Hegemony at Dalou

Princes at Ewin

Empire at Gloran

Domain at Yaumgan

Additional Alexandria Station Stories

The Story Road

Siren

Two Bottles of Wine With A War God

The Science Officer Series Season One

The Science Officer

The Mind Field

The Gilded Cage

The Pleasure Dome

The Doomsday Vault

The Last Flagship

The Hammerfield Gambit

The Hammerfield Payoff

The Bryce Connection

The Science Officer Series Season Two

Alien Seas

Buried Among the Stars

Captain Navarre

Last Stand

Lost Dreams

Ghost Towns

Games People Play

Prophet and Loss

Dandelion

Emergency

Warchild

Moot

Doomsday Girl

Princess

The Coven

Preacher Man

Captain Daring

Revoked

Returned

Reborn

The Lazarus Alliance

Escape

Return

Rebellion

Revolution

Liberation

Retribution

Alliance

Shadow of the Dominion

Longshot Hypothesis

Hard Bargain

Outermost

Dominion-427

Phoenix

Princess Rualoh

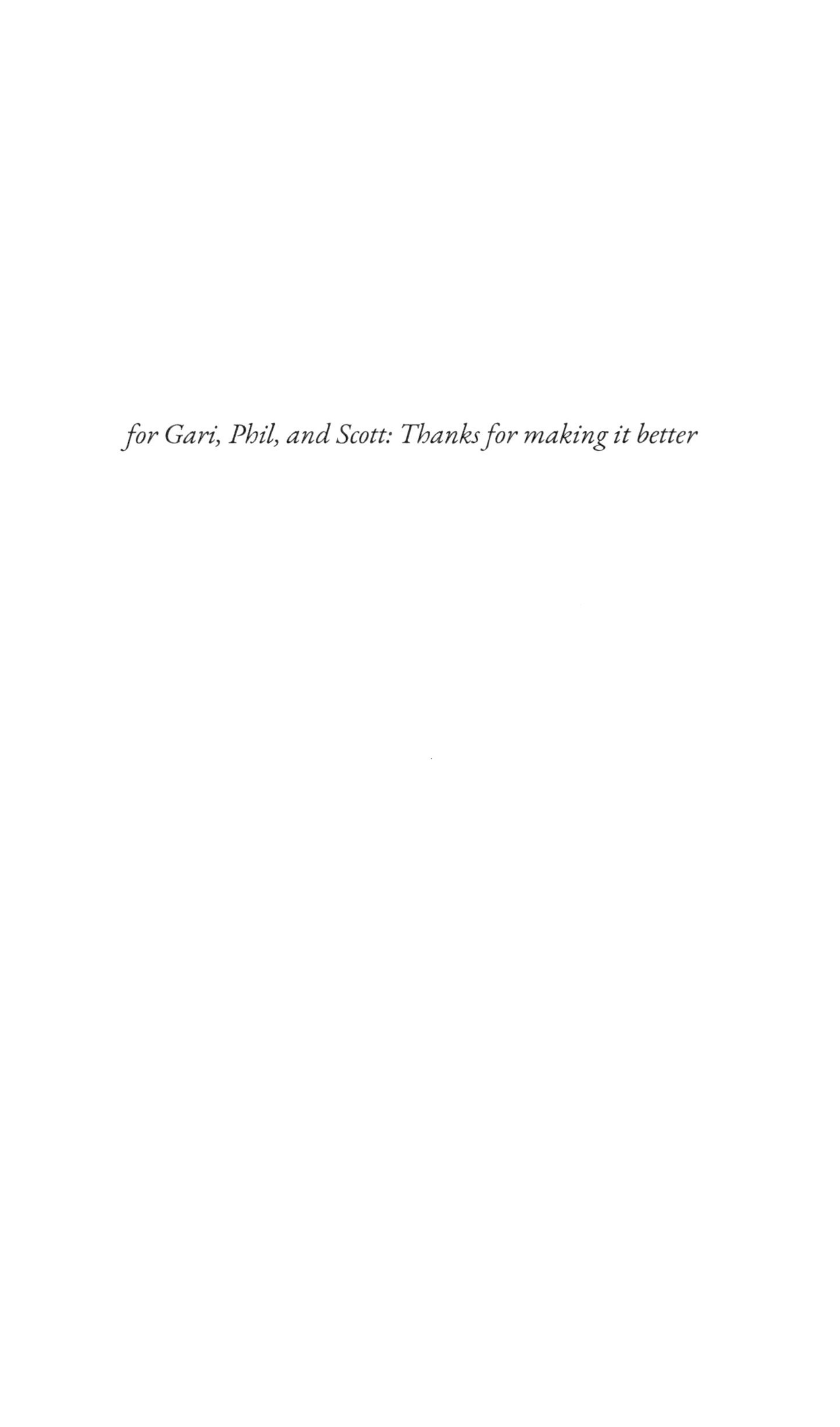

for Gari, Phil, and Scott: Thanks for making it better

PREFACE

Log: Directorate Cruiser, Tactical Transport
    Marrakesh (CTT)
Station: Albany, Belmark Region
Attached Special Mission Modules:
A) Advanced Weapons Testing
B) Survey, Type 2
Mission: Testing Borsheva Upgrades to Hv
    Particle Cannon System
Project: W93-O8F77R81
Security Clearance: 3+

1

———

"Weapons module, this is the Bridge," Captain Padraig Boru said into the open comm line as the second—and supposedly final—shot impacted on the distant asteroid. "Secure from firing while we evaluate your success."

"Understood, Captain," Dr. Borsheva replied coolly on the line.

That woman did everything coolly, which was fine. Padraig preferred it quiet and nerdy when playing with advanced new weapons technologies. Especially when blowing up random asteroids. Even in the middle of nowhere.

Padraig looked around his bridge. *DC Marrakesh* was an old ship. The *Cruiser, Tactical Transport* was older than most of its crew, pressed back into duty right at the moment it had been scheduled to be demobilized and retired to the Reserve Fleet. Maybe scrapped.

A new coat of paint, a new crew—most of whom were still kids, including him on some days—and the ship had been thrust back into service.

At least their first mission was something easy. He'd barely had time to take them out and do enough of a shakedown tour to make sure everything still worked before being called into dock and having those two modules plugged in.

Advanced Weapons Testing module for a new, experimental heavy particle cannon design. Survey module to make sure everything was working, with resolution of extremely fine detail at the sorts of long ranges that Dr. Borsheva's new invention promised.

Certainly, they'd come to rest one hell of a long ways out from that asteroid. And still blown it into three big pieces and a huge puff of plasma and fragments.

"Radio, what's it look like in the vicinity of the target?" Padraig called now.

Communications Officer Nyssa Taggart. Squire, or the *A'Zedi* Fleet's lowest commissioned officer rank. And one commissioned directly from her former rank as an enlisted Specialist, when someone had figured out how smart the young woman was. At nineteen, his youngest officer by several years, and his third youngest crew member.

Nyssa was a compact woman. Narrow shoulders, slender build, though still of medium height. Like everything had been squished inward. Incredibly smart, but not necessarily possessed of the sort of killer instinct that would put her in command of her own ship one of these days.

She looked up from her screen. Dark brown eyes in a face a shade darker than even the average for his crew. Brown hair always kept buzzed as short as regulations would allow.

If he'd permitted it, Padraig had no doubt Nyssa would get up every morning and shave her head like he shaved his whiskers. Might have to let her, one of these days, just to see.

Her face held confusion when she zeroed in on a feeling.

"Squire?" Padraig asked.

Grimace. Scowl. Something wasn't right, but Nyssa couldn't explain it.

But then, she possessed an esoteric magic when it came to sensors and communications. That was why she was Radio Officer.

Padraig played a hunch.

"Should I come over there to see?" he asked.

Nyssa lit up.

"Aye, sir!"

He rose and crossed. All his bridge officers and crew faced inward toward each other, with him at the center of the room. Made non-verbal communications better than having everyone lined up in rows facing forward, like the *United Technocracy of Wronlori* did it.

However, they were the enemy. Culturally as well as militarily.

Their sneak attack at *Eworn* two years ago had turned a hot peace into another conflict. *The War of the Fourth Alliance.* The *Sovereign Collective Directorate of A'Zedi*—his home—this time siding with the *Holy Imperium of Copez*, against *Wronlori*, with the *Enlightened Tyranny of Traisa* neutral at the moment and others on the sidelines hoping the storm blew a different direction.

Padraig moved to look over Nyssa's shoulder.

Two-dimensional screen plot, with colors and patterns indicating the third dimension and allowing her to rotate things with a trackball to shift her point of view.

Nyssa's finger came down on a point, clear at the edge of her screen. Almost a shadow, but closing, even if it was out more than three light-years yet.

"What is it?" he asked.

Padraig had his guesses, but it was her board.

"Inbound backtrack suggests a *Wronlori* origin, sir," Nyssa said quietly. "Nothing important back that direction, but if I wanted to slip into the Albany system at high speed, this is where I'd come from. Plus, we're out a ways from the planet Albany itself, and nobody normally sits at rest like this using Aetherial Sensors."

Padraig had to agree. The Aetherials were for navigation when you went to warp, bringing up the Ghostdrive to propel the ship to fast FTL.

But he'd ordered his Radio Officer to scan everything. Not her fault she'd taken him at his word. Whoever that was might have gotten almost on top of them before *Marrakesh* saw them.

"Have they picked us up yet?" he asked.

"Stand by," Nyssa replied.

He watched her work some more magic, typing in a quick formula and reading the results.

"Affirmative, Captain," Nyssa said firmly. "Target has deviated from their original flight plan that would have brought them out of warp close to Albany and are instead closing on *Marrakesh* at high FTL speed. Further, their Aetherial Sensor radiation suggests that the vessel is indeed of *Wronlori* manufacture."

Padraig studied the woman more than the message. Young, oh, so very young. Enlisted at seventeen. Commissioned as soon as she finished Radio School because everyone agreed she was by far the smartest student in her class. And the Directorate needed officers badly, still madly attempting to build up the fleet after the peace treaty negotiated eight years past had failed so badly two years ago.

Time wasted by politicians who had been convinced that *Wronlori* had finally seen the error of their ways. Hadn't helped when a new Archbishop had been proclaimed by the *Holy Imperium*, who then broke their previous treaty with *Wronlori* to join *A'Zedi* in an alliance. The Fourth Alliance, now that it was war again with *Wronlori*.

Nyssa Taggart was certain of her finding. Her eyes told him as much.

Padraig nodded and returned to his station, flipping up the little cover on his right-hand side to reveal the big red button underneath.

He slammed a fist into it and took a breath.

"All hands, this is Captain Boru," Padraig announced. "Stand by to receive enemy warship incursion."

2

———

Padraig reached under his station and pulled out the lifesuit he kept there. The bridge was at the core of *Marrakesh*, but it could still be hit by missile chunks or a particle cannon. Best to be prepared to lose atmosphere, even this deep inside.

Overhead, the lights took on a reddish tinge and an alarm siren wound up three times, paused, then sounded three more times. Sufficient to wake the dead.

"Bridge, this is Dr. Borsheva," she called from the module aft. "What should we do?"

Padraig nodded with a grimace, mostly to himself.

"Stand by your weapons, Doctor," he replied. "I may be calling on you to fire on an enemy vessel, in spite of our supposed secret mission to Albany to test your latest invention."

There was a pause before the woman spoke.

"Understood, Bridge," she said and then cut the line from her end.

Padraig opened the keypad and dialed the number for his Stevedore.

Kaitlin Lynch was the oldest crew member. After thirty years as an enlisted cargo specialist, she had happily retired as a Command Expert (E8) two years ago, after nearly a lifetime in *A'Zedi* purple. They'd asked her to return to duty but allowed her to serve as a civilian expert instead when she'd refused a commission. Her knowledge was that extraordinary.

"What's up, Padraig?" Kaitlin asked as she came on the line.

Informal. But she'd been enlisted crew for all her time, and was a retired—CIVILIAN—consultant today. She liked to remind everyone of that, in spite of her position as ship's Stevedore. Cargo controller for *Marrakesh*. Probably at least as important to him and his crew as his First Officer, Chance Messier.

However, she didn't do spit and polish anymore. If she ever had.

"Nyssa thinks it's a *Wronlori* incursion," Padraig replied simply. "I agree, so we're going to combat footing. You get to babysit the civilians—the *other civilians*—and help them deal with firing that big turret if we have to."

He could hear the smile in her voice when she replied.

"Already on station," Kaitlin replied. "Got my people shadowing hers. Figure we should swap crews out?"

"Your call, Kaitlin," Padraig said. "If it gets hot and heavy, a pair of extreme range, experimental heavy particle cannons would be a nice surprise. I can't imagine someone racing madly over here if they didn't know where we were already. And who they were looking for."

"Someone big enough to threaten *Marrakesh*?" she asked.

"Always err short of the cliff, woman," he replied with a laugh, throwing her own favorite quote back in her face. "I seem to remember someone telling me that a time or two."

As Stevedore, she was responsible for getting special mission modules installed and removed, then making sure they synchronized with the ship, both physically as well as socially, since most of them came with their own crews who might not be military folks used to life on a warship.

Like Dr. Borsheva and her team.

Academics, the lot of them. Nice folks. Probably never been shot at. Stevedores had to move with patience.

Kaitlin laughed back and cut the line.

"Nyssa, time to intercept?" Padraig asked, looking around to see that folks had their own lifesuits out and handy.

"Estimate six minutes, Captain," she replied.

"Everyone take thirty seconds and suit up," Padraig ordered.

He had mostly officers and senior enlisted with him right now. Luck of timing, as he'd wanted his experts keeping track of Borsheva's test. Normally, it would be about half and half.

If trouble was coming, this timing had saved him several minutes of mental adjustment for folks. otherwise

Padraig decided to play another hunch. He keyed in a different number on the keypad.

"Engineering. Ahearn."

Knight Jareth Ahearn. Senior officer back there, in charge of the Ghostdrives, the rotary thrusters, and all his power systems. A good, calm man at the best of times, as well as the worst of times.

Today might be either.

"This is Boru," Padraig replied. "Go ahead and reconfigure the Ghostdrive for operation. Might be needing it shortly."

"Is he running or us?" Ahearn asked with a sharp, interested voice.

"I'll let you know as soon as he arrives," Padraig replied with a lilt. "Got a party crasher right now."

"Understood, sir," Ahearn replied. "Bringing some generators online now. Give me…eight minutes to stabilize."

Padraig nodded and cut the line. Ghostdrives took a little time to warm up when you hadn't been using them. Still, they could safely throw you up into a slightly different plane of existence where distances were somehow closer together, letting you fly at a fast FTL while still being able to see the normal space you fell out from. Aetherial Sensors let you look across that boundary as well. Weapons could even be used, if you got right on top of the other vessel, but Ghost-space made the effects wonky at the best of times.

It was even possible to send ultra-high-speed messages home, but they would take hours or days to get there.

Marrakesh was on its own today.

And trouble was coming.

Padraig looked to his Weapons Officer, Armiger Maddox Nevin. Fourth generation sailor, but first generation as an officer.

"Nevin, are your gun crews ready?" Padraig asked.

"Affirmative, sir," Nevin replied with a nod. "I had them all on duty already, in case we needed to blow up any stray rubble that threatened the ship. Or if I could convince you to close with the asteroid for a firing drill."

Padraig nodded and smiled. The job of handling the big guns was always for someone aggressive, but Nevin tempered it well. Always training. Always thinking ahead. Always prepared. Reminded Padraig of his own days as Gunner, back on *Nemesis*.

Padraig started slipping the lifesuit over his uniform, leaving the helmet hung over the side of his chair by the lanyard. A light on his panel told him that his First Officer was on station in the Secondary Bridge.

There wasn't much left to do but be prepared. He'd gotten a pretty good crew from the Bureau of Personnel, but they'd only been together for six months now, loading and testing the ship before a first shakedown cruise. Then a quick hop to load modules before flying out to Albany in the middle of nowhere.

They would normally need more time to gel, but he'd just run out of everything.

Nyssa's countdown clock clicked over to one minute to incursion.

3

———

Padraig had a small screen on his left-hand side echoing the feed from Nyssa Taggart. She was doing an excellent job of tracking the bogey inbound, then caught it with a sensor ping as soon as they dropped into real space.

"Crap, that's a Leviathan," somebody muttered in the suddenly silent bridge.

Padraig had to agree with that sentiment. *Marrakesh* was built on a cruiser hull, though without that weapons module aft they were normally hardly more armed than a frigate. Tactical Transports had a different job in the fleet than fighting.

With the module, they were comparable to most cruisers, though still on the lower end.

But most cruisers still wouldn't stand a chance against a *Wronlori* Leviathan. Capital ship. Mothership, at that, with four gunboats carried parasite-style inside. The Leviathan's wolfpack could probably take *Marrakesh* by themselves.

The Leviathan wouldn't really need help.

"Gun teams, open up with the heavy particle cannons, but hold the missiles in the launch tubes," Padraig ordered.

"Weapons module, fire as you bear. Engineering, we need to run. Helm, ahead full on this heading with everything you've got, then prepare for transition to Ghostdrive as soon as Ahearn gives you the clearance."

Zarah Halloran, Squire, had the helm. Young officer. *Three days out of Uni* was her running joke, but she had really only been commissioned barely in time to join *Marrakesh*'s crew for this shakedown cruise, so it wasn't entirely a joke.

Everyone was stretching themselves into new jobs. Padraig hadn't expected to be promoted to Captain for several more years. But the war had come, and the fleet suddenly needed people and hulls. Anybody and anything they could get.

Padraig had too many ninety-day-wonders among his officers for his own comfort. Civilians with degrees put into a high-pressure training environment when they enlisted to give them the tools they needed to survive. Halloran had at least come out of Fleet University, so she had one step up on them.

She nodded to herself and began to toggle keys like a concert pianist.

A'Zedi didn't trust automation like *Wronlori* did. Ships were mechanical, because tying everything to a single computer system meant that a point-source-failure left you stranded. Maybe doomed.

Not a good place to be in deep space.

Wronlori had a smaller population base than everyone else, so they were willing to take those chances as a culture.

Aft, the rotary thrusters cut loose with a vibration Padraig could feel in his sternum. The direction didn't matter all that much, as he had no intention of maneuvering to duel with a *Wronlori* squadron that could tear him apart.

Flashes of light on Taggart's echoed screen told him that

the Leviathan had opened fire. They had more heavy particle cannons in turrets, intended to stand in line of battle to fight.

Marrakesh wasn't turned broadside to the enemy warship, but the aft turret had two hundred and seventy degrees of firing arc to slew around, Parthian-style, and it was enough. Four shots flashed out in rapid succession. One even hit, from the way the Leviathan suddenly erupted in plasma.

"First blood," Nevin said proudly from his Weapons Officer station.

More luck than anything, but Padraig would always take luck over skill.

You could be good, but the other captain might get lucky…

"Nicely done, Gunner," Padraig said, smiling at the man.

Marrakesh's hull rang like a bell in response.

"Engineering?" Padraig called.

Even at this range, heavy particle cannons had one hell of a thump. Missiles were more effective, but *Marrakesh* wasn't staying around to provide guidance for them.

"Thirty seconds, Captain," Ahearn said over the line. "It'll be rough, but I don't figure you'll care all that much."

"Indeed, Ahearn," Padraig said. "Just get us gone. Secondary Bridge, how's damage control?"

Chance answered immediately, her voice crisp and sound.

"Took a slash down the starboard side," she replied. "Below the regular gun turrets and trailing low off the hull. Armor took most of it and penetrations are minimal at present. We've closed off four chambers until we can repair them."

Padraig nodded. Heavies, at range. You couldn't blow up most ships with particle beams. That was what the missiles were for, having time to accelerate to high speed before splitting down into ship-killing components impacting at a measurable fraction of light speed.

One of those might punch starlight through a Leviathan.

"Radio, is the Leviathan deploying parasite craft?" Padraig asked.

"Negative at present, Captain," Taggart replied. "I'm keeping watch. What does it mean that launching parasite vessels wasn't the first thing they did?"

"It means that they expect us to run and don't want to pause to gather up their wolfpack to chase us down," Padraig replied.

Part of his job was teaching his young crew, though he was hardly the most seasoned veteran around here. At thirty-four, he was only two years senior to Chance Messier.

Still, he had the most experience on warships, not counting Kaitlin.

Young officers. Young crew. Old ship. New war.

Needs must, when the devil drives.

A second outbound salvo included those experimental beams that Borsheva had invented. One of those scored a solid hit, because the plasma cloud Taggart picked up was larger this time.

"Sir, that might have hit a gunboat in bay," Nyssa called. "The scan places it close to the launch cradle for the forward starboard bay on the schematics."

Padraig nodded. Good and bad. One fewer gunboat later, assuming that they had to stop and repair it. At the same time, if the Leviathan wasn't about to deploy, then he'd prefer hits on their main hull. Maybe knock out a cannon.

Marrakesh normally had twin heavies in each of two turrets, one forward and one aft. The Leviathan had a stacked pair of triple turrets at each end. Twelve barrels to his four. And brought bigger guns.

Borsheva's experimental module had better range, but they

were too close to the enemy warship for that to matter right now.

Then Ahearn got things aligned and *Marrakesh* went into Ghost-space with a bright blink and a harder lurch than was normal.

Still, they were away.

Or, at least, running for their lives.

4

"Radio, what's their status?" Padraig called as *Marrakesh* lit out at FTL speeds.

The bow had been pointed not quite on a reciprocal to the Leviathan, but close enough for navigation.

She paused for several seconds, watching her boards.

"The enemy vessel has also transitioned to Ghostdrive, Captain," Nyssa replied crisply, though he could hear the excitement and concern in her voice. "Currently, they are in pursuit."

Padraig nodded.

Somebody over there had been expecting him to run immediately. Wise, considering the mismatch in size and firepower. They'd had to slew around first, though, since *Marrakesh* had blown by them at high speed.

At the same time, how in the Seven Hells had they known someone would be on station near Albany? Wasn't like that Leviathan had cruised in slowly and carefully before committing. No, they'd come in fast and landed close enough to

Marrakesh to open fire almost immediately. Like they knew who he was. And where.

That suggested a leak somewhere. Or a code had been broken that allowed the ship over there to know where *Marrakesh* was, and what they were up to.

He keyed open the ship-wide intercom.

"All hands, this is Captain Boru," he announced slowly. "We have transitioned to Ghostdrive. Remain alert, but you may relax one notch while we sort out what our next steps are. Wardrooms, expect to serve the crew their meals in place and plan accordingly."

He cut the line and studied the plot Taggart had going.

"Radio, what's the relative velocity and rate of closure?" Padraig asked.

"Mark Six, Captain," she replied instantly. "The Leviathan is closing at Six point One, but the gap was not that wide to begin with."

Six light-years per hour. Fast FTL, but not fast enough, it seemed. Not surprising, since the larger the ship, the more power they generally had available for Ghostdrives.

Plus, the captain over there had been prepared. Was probably pushing his own ship and crew to maintain the chase and slowly overtake *Marrakesh*.

Technically, it was possible to fight while using Ghostdrives. Beams could be used if you got inside one light-second. And were desperate. And got lucky. Missiles fell back into NAFAL—sublight speeds—instantly and were irrelevant.

So, that Leviathan could chase them. Padraig assumed that they probably had more fuel reserves as well, so eventually he might be forced to fight, either here or there. Or be left stranded in the middle of nowhere.

Why would *Wronlori* send a Leviathan after *Marrakesh*? An old Tactical Transport like this was hardly worth all the effort.

Unless someone knew that Alexis Borsheva was aboard.

That thought chilled Padraig more than the first glimpse of that Leviathan on Taggart's screen.

They were starting to accumulate far too many coincidences here for his comfort.

Sure, the woman was famous. Was she that dangerous, at least in *Wronlori*'s eyes?

"Engine Room, this is the Captain," Padraig said as he called them. "Are we stable in flight for now?"

"Affirmative, sir," Ahearn replied. "Ship got fully tuned for recommissioning, and this is the first time we've pushed anything."

"Very good, Ahearn," Padraig replied. "Stay on top of it."

He switched channels.

"Secondary Bridge. Messier."

"You have command for now," Padraig told her. "I'm going aft to talk to Kaitlin and Dr. Borsheva. Keep running for now and have Nyssa Taggart figure out what that other ship's plans are. Questions?"

"Negative, Padraig," Chance replied. "On it."

He cut the line.

"Taggart," he called, getting Nyssa to look up from the screens she had been tracking so intently. "You're on point here. Look ahead of us and see where we are headed and where we can run. Any terrain we can use to escape them or at least force them to back off or lose ground. I'll be back in a bit and you'll brief me. Call on whatever resources you need, whoever you need, with priority. Am I clear?"

She gulped once, eyes huge, then nodded.

He watched the young woman lock in and focus, fingers typing commands with sharp authority.

Padraig nodded and headed aft towards the hatch.

5

Padraig entered the sensors module after confirming where everyone was. The weapons themselves, along with generators and control systems for them, were in the other module, with both crews bunking here for the most part.

Dr. Borsheva was up and forward, standing next to Kaitlin and several techs when he entered the main control space for the guns overhead.

Padraig looked around, then nodded both women to a nearby conference room.

"We're in mad flight right now," he told them. "Let's take a few minutes and regroup."

Borsheva grimaced and followed. Kaitlin Lynch had a thoughtful, questioning look, but remained silent and trailed them into the office.

Padraig sat on the near side and gestured for the other two to join him.

"We might have a problem," he announced simply when the hatch closed, studying Alexis Borsheva, PhD.

Medium height, with dark skin a shade this side of

bronze, but hair bleached white then tinted down into a strawberry pink that Padraig found weird. Nice looking, but odd.

Forty Standard, give or take, so he supposed she might be dyeing out the inevitable grays.

Brilliant dark eyes followed him as he gestured to the ship around them.

"The enemy Leviathan acts as if they knew there would be a ship at Albany worth attacking immediately on arriving," Padraig began.

Kaitlin gasped quietly, but she'd been in that purple uniform for thirty years, so she understood what level of planning something like that required.

"Okay?" Dr. Borsheva replied with confusion when he waited for her to process.

"When they detected us, they also immediately changed course and charged," Padraig continued.

Again, Kaitlin stirred, but remained quiet. She understood where he was going.

"Finally, someone sent a Leviathan to Albany," Padraig said, "which is a poor world on the fringe of everything and everyone. Hardly big enough to have a dock *Marrakesh* could use, and not a military target of any kind. Local defenses would be enough to drive off a Leviathan with their own gunboat swarms, but the Leviathan immediately attacked us, then gave chase."

It sunk in. Borsheva's eyes got big, then angry.

"They knew we were here," she said. "That I was here, possibly."

"That's my thought as well, Doctor," Padraig said. "I can send a message to Fleet Headquarters, but it will take at least two days to get any useful response, and there's not much they can do except consign us to our doom or congratulate us on escaping trouble."

"The security failings that would let *Wronlori* know she was aboard *Marrakesh* are immense," Kaitlin spoke up now. "Do we have a leak aboard?"

"I doubt it," Padraig replied, turning to her. "Just the amount of time to route a warship like that after us here suggests that they read our orders almost as quickly as we did, if not before. I'm guessing it was at the other end. Either someone in her organization or a spy at home leaked. I'll send a package report in a little while, then update it as we go, but I wanted you two to know."

"Should I bring in a security team?" Kaitlin asked. "Protect Dr. Borsheva against assassination, since their first swoop to capture us failed?"

Padraig considered it. Sound logic, all the way around, except that it might provoke an assassin to move immediately.

He studied the good doctor.

She studied him back. The woman was a few shades smarter than Nyssa Taggart when it came to pure intellectual firepower, which said something. Patents, professional articles, and a list of inventions.

If you had a high enough security clearance to know. Most of the ship's crew didn't even rate that high. Him, Kaitlin, and Chance, probably.

"Dr. Borsheva, at present, is there anything you can contribute to your team, in terms of actually using those new weapons?" Padraig asked. "I'm aware that you were present to supervise and study results in real time, but that is no longer the most important thing happening today."

"You are correct, Captain," Borsheva replied.

He turned to his Stevedore now, speaking carefully.

"Cargo Control is your job, Kaitlin," Padraig said, emphasizing that he was on her terrain right now, in spite of being captain of the ship.

Kaitlin nodded warily.

Civilian. Older woman. *Expert.*

Easy to tread on her toes wrong and he needed her probably more than anyone else aboard, if he wanted *Marrakesh* to run smoothly.

"I might suggest that you remove Dr. Borsheva to the main ship," Padraig said. "For her own safety, and just in case someone in one of the modules isn't who they seem."

He could order it. Captains were functionally gods aboard their own vessel. However, Kaitlin Lynch was among the best he'd ever met at the job. And Cargo Control really was her responsibility.

Better to draw her in than alienate her by taking over.

"Agreed," Kaitlin nodded.

Then she rose and moved to the intercom controls by the door, dialing in a number.

"Secondary Bridge. Messier."

"Lynch here," Kaitlin said. "I'm going to send Dr. Borsheva aft. Please attach a security team directly to her for safety, then lock down both modules with armed teams at the main hatches that only answer to orders from yourself, me, and Captain Boru."

There was a hint of a pause, but Chance was a sharp woman as well.

"Understood," she said, figuring that Padraig would explain it when she saw him.

"Very good," Kaitlin said, cutting the line.

She returned to the table and sat. Borsheva had gone a little pale around the edges.

"Really?" she asked, voice breathless.

"I'd rather you be safe and me look overprotective than be sorry I didn't protect you, Doctor," Padraig nodded. "All of this smells to high heaven, as far as I'm concerned."

"Can you outrun them?" Borsheva asked.

"For now," he replied, standing. "That will change at some point, and we might have to fight."

"So, what should I do?" the scientist asked.

Padraig turned to Kaitlin. "I want you to take over command of both modules and both teams. Gunnery, sensors, damage control, everything. I'm willing to add more crew in to help but not to pull out anyone until we can vet them. Understood?"

"You got it," she nodded. "I have the people I need, but a damage control party would be helpful in case something goes wrong. I've got engineers to handle the hardware. Keeping the hull intact is my only weakness at present."

"Let Chance know," he nodded back, then turned to Borsheva. "Doctor, if you would accompany me?"

He got her out into the main room quickly, watching the few folks in sight like a hawk as they headed to the main hatch.

"Consultations aft," he announced, mostly to muddy the waters in case someone wanted to pull a weapon before she could escape them.

Borsheva made it to the main hatch and exited, with Padraig close behind her.

He paused to key the intercom.

"Chance, we're out," he said. "Lock them in."

The light next to the door turned red in response.

"It is really that necessary, Captain?" Borsheva asked.

"It might be," Padraig replied.

6

———

Kaitlin looked around her new fiefdom. It was her old domain, but she'd been pleasantly surprised when Padraig put her fully in command and gave her free rein. And reinforced it just now.

He might still be a kid in her eyes, but someone along the line had trained him right. She approved.

And she *could* call him a kid, being almost twenty years older. She didn't have any children herself, but that had been a personal choice early on, one that had let her see the galaxy.

Later, nobody interesting had come along who would have made her change her mind.

Today, she was the boss.

She looked around the group and smiled.

Den Gilroy was her Docker on *Marrakesh*. Senior Enlisted crew in the cargo section, responsible for the pods.

Her old job, before Fleet had convinced her to sign on as a civilian contractor at triple the pay she'd have made merely returning to duty. Not that she needed the income, as she'd had little to spend it on besides spoiling nieces and nephews, and their little ones, but it put her in charge.

That was good.

Den had a concerned look on his face, which that was probably because of the smile on hers. The civilians around the space didn't understand navy procedures well enough to worry.

"Captain's locking the ship down for combat and damage control," Kaitlin lied persuasively to everyone. "We're to remain isolated in here until the situation outside the ship is resolved."

Den stirred but held his tongue. Which was wise on his part.

"What about Alexis?" one of the techs asked.

Another kid. Civilian. Postdoctoral student, but still a kid, even if he was in his late twenties.

Everybody on the ship felt like kids to her.

Her kids, though, even the strangers.

"She's going to be consulting with our engine room folks about how to use the power off the module," Kaitlin nodded, still spinning yarns. Still, believable ones if you didn't wear purple like her people. Her own people knew she was up to something. And knew to keep their mouths shut. "Then they are going to see about integrating the turret above us if we have to fight."

Den nodded. That much he believed, since they had an experimental heavy particle cannon turret. And a Leviathan they might need to use it on.

"What should we be doing?" the post-doc kid asked.

Smart lad. Kinda cute. Way too young for her.

Still, Kaitlin smiled at him anyway.

"Whatever maintenance you need to do if we're about to start firing the turret as quickly as the cooling systems and generators can handle the load," she replied. "If it comes to battle, that's going to be critical."

She watched as the man turned to several others, mostly older and techs instead of boffins, and the group moved. Stairs would take them up to the weapons, but they started going down first, to where the banks of batteries and generators were located.

Kaitlin looked around at her people.

"You, too," she said in a soft voice that still had the steel fist contained inside.

Most of them moved, headed out to start checking fuel loads and wear.

Den was the only one who stayed put. She wasn't surprised.

"That was as pretty a load of horseshit as I think I've ever heard, Kaitlin," he murmured with a smile. "What's really going on?"

"Keep this under your hat," she said, face turning hard. "Padraig worries that there was a leak somewhere that let *Wronlori* know who we were and where. And that there might be someone on Borsheva's team who isn't what they seem."

"Threat to her?" Den perked up.

He was a short man, like her. Compact. Fourteen centimeters taller. Massive shoulders and arms. Good *feng shui* on the tattoos that peeked out from his sleeves. Supposedly, the man was covered in ink, though she'd never seen it. Muscles on top of muscles.

"Padraig removed her to someplace safe, and she won't be back," Kaitlin nodded. "Nobody leaves. A damage control team will be routed in, then trapped with us. Let our people know to keep their mouths shut about the change in standard procedures so they don't give it away."

Den nodded and headed towards the stairs.

Kaitlin wanted to race after the man, to get her hands dirty and oily keeping everything in tip-top shape. However, she was management now, so she had to curb that impulse. Instead, she headed to her office. She was familiar with the new weapons systems, since she was Stevedore and this was her department.

Kaitlin still wanted to review a few things.

Their lives might depend on it.

7

Chance Messier looked up when the hatch opened and the captain strode in, their guest close on his heels. Padraig was tall and skinny. Made a good match with Kaitlin Lynch, who was short, broad, and probably one of the strongest people on the vessel after her Docker, Dennie Gilroy.

Chance was in the middle. Above average height. Average build tending to curvy if she didn't religiously spend time on the machines and watch her caloric intake. Black hair, but straight.

Husband and two kids back home, which she knew was odd in the Fleet, but Robin was happy being a househusband, so it worked. And Daneel, her youngest, was old enough that she could get back to sailing after several years behind a desk.

Felt good to be in space again.

Captain came to rest nearby and gestured Dr. Borsheva into a nearby station, currently locked and mostly powered down. He sat next to her then looked around the entire Secondary Bridge.

Everybody was in purple and emergency suits, which seemed to be what he was looking for.

"I may be overreacting," Captain said simply. "If so, I'll own that later. The situation doesn't add up."

"Leviathan knowing where to find us, then being ready to immediately give chase when we ran like hell?" Chance asked.

She'd been doing the maths herself.

"Exactly," Captain nodded. "To be extra cautious while fighting an enemy warship big enough to take us, I have ordered Dr. Borsheva to remove herself from the two modules. She will bunk and sup with the crew for now. Nobody else leaves either module unless you, me, or Kaitlin orders it. I do not know if there is an assassin in her group. Nor do I wish to find out."

"We intending to fight the Leviathan?" Chance asked.

That was really the important factor here. Big son of a bitch back there chasing them.

"Might not be our decision, Chance," he replied with a nod. "I want you and Dr. Borsheva to go over the capabilities and limitations of her systems, in case it comes to that. I'm returning to the bridge forward and looking for ways we can evade."

"They are closing, but slowly," she informed him. "We probably have one hundred and fifty minutes or so until they are close enough to consider engaging us with particle cannon, even in Ghost-space."

Captain nodded again. Ugly situation. She'd been sitting here trying to think of something to help, but they were at the ass-end of beyond right now. Unclaimed and largely unexplored space that direction. A few places colonized but nothing important or hardly even relevant.

And that Leviathan on their asses.

"We'll be doing everything we can to avoid them. Assume we'll be firing as soon as they get close enough or drop into space with us," he ordered now. "Get me optimum engagement ranges, firing rates, and how far we can push the hardware if we have to. Remember, all of this is a tool. The crew is the people aboard, and we can use up all the hardware, as long as we get everyone home afterwards."

Captain exited and Chance nodded, smiling at Dr. Borsheva. She'd eaten meals with the woman and toured the modules to understand things but not really spent much time either professional or personal with her.

That looked to change starting now.

"So, Doc," Chance began. "What can you tell me about stinging beasts from the deep?"

8

———

Padraig entered the bridge and took his station.

"Chance, I have the bridge," he said, calling aft.

"All yours," Chance replied.

He looked around.

"Taggart, Chance tells me that they will overhaul us in about one hundred and fifty minutes?" he began, watching the young woman who had already saved their asses at least once today. Maybe twice.

And the day was still young.

"Affirmative, Captain," she nodded. "Current call is one fifty-four, but that depends on how hard each of us pushes our Ghostdrives at this stage."

He nodded and dialed a number.

"Ahearn."

"What's your status on speed, Jareth?" Padraig asked.

"Already pushing things as close to the edge as I dare, sir," the engineer replied. "Not sure how soon before something breaks at my end and they're right on top of us."

"You are encouraged to use up resources, Jareth," Padraig

39

reminded him. "And we're likely fresher out of a full yard refit than they are, so we ought to be better able to walk out on that ledge. And for longer."

"Understood, sir," he replied. "Lemme consult with my chickadees and see if we can eke out another percent or three back here."

Padraig cut the line and nodded to the nervous faces staring back at him.

Command right now involved maintaining a calm presence that let them work without panic. Everyone here was a volunteer, though many were still raw around the edges, sailors on their first ever deployment suddenly facing a potential fight to the death.

He'd been there. Both recently as well as in the last war, when he'd been a pup aboard the Line Cruiser *Nemesis*, itself almost as old as *Marrakesh*, though his ship was the last of the old *M-boats* still in service, as far as he knew.

A couple had been activated out of the Reserve Fleet, but those were slower to come online. *Marrakesh* had been ready to serve.

He turned his attention to Armiger Nevin next.

"Nevin, you head aft now and join Chance and Dr. Borsheva," he ordered. "They are doing a full review of the new weapons systems and how to use them. You need to be listening so you can communicate with your crews."

Maddox Nevin nodded, locked his station, and moved quickly.

Normally, someone else would move to the station, but the gun crews were already in their turrets and could fight without coordination from here. And Nevin would be with Chance on the Secondary Bridge if they did have to slug it out.

He needed other options.

"Helm, what's your status?" he asked.

After all, his original orders had been to move away from trouble, rather than going somewhere in particular.

Zarah Halloran looked at him with a hint of panic in her eyes, like this was a pop quiz she hadn't studied for.

Every day might be a pop quiz.

"Our original path was the luck of the solar wind at the moment of insertion, Captain," she replied, gulping and focusing. "Down thirteen degrees from the galactic ecliptic plane itself."

"What's in front of us?" he asked.

Getting away from destruction had been more important. That was changing.

Halloran looked over at Nyssa Taggart, and some unspoken conversation occurred. Good.

"I've been reviewing survey records, sir," Nyssa spoke up now. "There are several solar systems in our forward cone. None are known to be inhabited at present."

"Anywhere we can hide?" he asked.

They didn't need long. Just enough to open sufficient space on the Leviathan, then vanish into the dark somehow. If the Leviathan got too close, they had to risk getting the surprise reversed on them.

He'd be okay with that, too.

Nyssa grimaced and Zarah Halloran spoke next.

"There is a planet-forming nebula," she said. "Down a bit more and out a ways. Young, in that there are only a handful of blue stars formed so far, with others in various stages of collapse before forming new solar systems."

"How far out?" Padraig asked.

Anything that would buy them time. If *Marrakesh* had been closer to home, he could have run that way, but they were a week out from the nearest fleet base, and running at high speed like this would burn all their fuel long before they got someplace safe.

"The nearest edge is just under one hundred and twenty light-years away, sir," Nyssa replied.

It was a strange way to have a conversation, but the two women were obviously working well together. Better than he'd expected, this early in a deployment.

It gave him hope.

Padraig considered the distance. And the risks.

"Change course," he ordered both women. "Aim us at the densest part of the cloud and maintain current speed. Then talk to Ahearn and see if we can push harder. I need Six point One maintained, so they remain aft far enough. Get me to the nebula."

"What does that gain us, sir?" Nyssa asked, eyes almost crossed with confusion.

"How well do your sensors work in a nebula like that, Squire?" he asked with a grin.

"Not for shit, sir," she replied, then slapped a hand over her mouth and turned so beet red he thought she might pass out.

Or maybe want to die of embarrassment.

Padraig grinned at her.

"And we have a full Survey module docked aft, Taggart," he reminded her. "That ought to let us see them better than they can see us, especially if both of us drop to passive reads only to try and hide."

"Why would they go passive, sir?" Zarah asked.

"Because they won't know exactly where we are, even if they get close," he said. "A few light-seconds is still a huge sphere, if they can't see anything. And a nebula will play merry hell with particle cannons, so both of us probably have to rely on missiles to engage. The moment they launch their wolfpack, we can run again, and they'd have to pause while retrieving everything. I'm guessing such an action buys us as much as an hour, depending on the quality of their crews. We can possibly get out of scanner range entirely in that period. Then we've escaped."

"So, it handicaps them far more than us, sir?" Nyssa lit up with a smile.

"Exactly, sailor," he said. "You work with the folks in the Survey module to understand exactly what our options are, but they are to remain confined to the module for now."

"Sir?" she asked.

"Operational security, Taggart," he said.

"Aye, sir."

"Oh, and Taggart?" he said. "You will be in command of all the scanner equipment when this happens."

Her eyes got big again, then the young woman seemed to shrink in a bit. Except that she was squaring herself. Settling. Focusing.

A different woman looked out of those eyes a moment later.

"Aye, sir," Nyssa said crisply.

Padraig smiled.

The Leviathan had made at least one mistake. As long as *Marrakesh* didn't make any, he might yet pull this off.

9

—————

Padraig studied the remains of his dinner. Nothing fancy, as the kitchen had rolled a cart in and handed out covered meals around the room. Pasta in a pinkish sauce, with meatballs and garlic bread on the side. Easy to make in huge loads, then dump into bowls and put on a roller cart.

As Captain, he could have gone back and gotten his dinner in the wardroom, but he needed to be here on the bridge. With his people.

Too many youngsters who hadn't ever been in a situation like this, most of them patriots drawn to enlist by the surprise attack on Eworn nearly two years ago. And ninety-day-wonders still learning how to be officers and leaders.

Even Chance had been flying a desk for several years, until Xandra and Daneel were both finally old enough.

All the weight of *Marrakesh* was on his shoulders, for good or ill.

The examples he set for his people today would stay with them for the rest of their careers, whether that would be four-and-out, or thirty and retired, like Kaitlin Lynch.

45

As a result, he had sat at his station and only spilled one drip down the front of his emergency suit as he ate. Like about half the people he could see.

Folks had started to rotate on and off watch, though most of them had only gone so far as the nearest sleeping coffin, those stacked just off the bridge for exactly this sort of situation.

Some Captains believed that they should keep their first team on duty for twelve or eighteen hours in a crisis, but again, Padraig was setting expectations for the next two generations of officers. Those he trained now and the ones they trained later.

Had there been an expectation of battle shortly, he might have done it differently, but they were still twelve hours out from the nebula, Ahearn having managed to get them to Six point One One, that extra bit. They'd even opened the gap a shade, then the Leviathan had moved heaven and earth and managed to hold on.

Marrakesh was a rabbit in the high grass with the hounds sniffing and baying. Or maybe a coyote, since he could fight back even better than a fox could.

Right now, Nyssa and Zarah had both taken a break to eat, then nap. Andrea Whelan had the helm, though he had teased her just a little bit about that.

The woman was the senior-most enlisted crew member aboard. The *Coxswain* herself, though she maintained all her watch-sitting certifications. Hell, Whelan could probably do just about any job on this ship—including his—save maybe some of the finer points of engineering that Jareth Ahearn or Roderic Garber, the Carpenter or Chief Engineering Enlisted crew member aft, might still be better at.

Maybe.

Padraig caught the eye of the young man next to Whelan.

Specialist Glen Tameron, currently sitting on Radio with Nyssa hopefully sleeping.

"Status of the enemy warship, Tameron?" Padraig asked.

The man had eaten just before coming on duty, so he was focused. Padraig needed that right now.

"They're holding steady at roughly fifteen light-seconds, dead astern, sir," he said. "Each time we've adjusted our course, they have shaved a little distance off by cutting the chord of our arc, but we're currently running straight and true."

Padraig nodded.

Stern chase. The hardest thing to escape from if the enemy was committed.

And he had no way of knowing their own fuel status for running at these speeds. Inefficient, because this was an emergency run, when normal sailing stayed under two light-years per hour.

Still, they'd started it, so he had to assume they were prepared to see it through.

"At some point, Specialist, they may try to close in tighter," Padraig told the man. "Once they realize that we're going to try to lose them in the nebula. We'll be aiming for the kinds of fog that might hide us, so they may try to burn out their engines and overhaul us short of that. If they start closing, sound the alarm immediately."

"Aye, sir," Tameron replied. "Cox said something along those lines when I came on duty."

Padraig nodded thanks to the Chief. Her sitting a watch now gave all the rest of his officers more confidence that they could sleep, at least for a little while.

And he could stay sharp for at least thirty hours awake. He'd done that enough times, though he wasn't the crazy punk he'd been at twenty anymore.

Padraig leaned back as stewards began collecting plates and bowls. Rather than retire to an office, he brought up an echo of Tameron's rear-facing scans on his own tiny screen.

Leviathan. *Wronlori*'s concept of a Space Control Ship. Wolfpack of four gunships carried docked, parasite style. Bigger guns and a greater range than most cruisers.

But only most, since *Marrakesh* had the turret of the experimental jobbies up top.

Still, like a shark, trailing them in the water.

He wondered what they were thinking.

10

BRIDGE, SUNDERING WRATH

Marshal Divna Babic stood next to the ship's Captain and studied the wide screen at the front of the large command space. It had the plot of the fleeing experimental tug cruiser ahead of them, as seen from an overhead view by some omniscient being. As Marshal in command of the Leviathan *Sundering Wrath*, she was in charge of this operation.

It had been bad luck that they had been seen at the edge of scanner range by the *A'Zedi* ship. Timing, she presumed, due to whatever firing experiments they had been conducting with the new systems that damnable scientist Borsheva had invented this time.

Marrakesh had fled, with *Sundering Wrath* caught facing the wrong direction and unable to attack effectively. Hounding them now, Divna hoped that they might make a mistake.

It was that or chase the smaller vessel while it fled someplace until she could get close enough to engage in Ghost-space.

She had hoped to trap them at Albany, then damage the vessel sufficiently that they could not escape her fury. For now, the pursuit was taking them deeper into unknown regions of space. At least unknown to *Sundering Wrath*'s crew.

Divna stopped studying the wall and turned to *Sundering Wrath*'s captain, Dragutin Maric. Tall, as *Wronlori* males tended to be compared to other star nations. Light skin, compared to *A'Zedi*. Hair almost blond.

Rather like her.

"Status of *Marrakesh*?" she asked.

He looked down at the various boards showing departments. Divna could have read all of it herself, as it hadn't been that long ago when she'd been a Captain, but this was his ship. His people.

Her mission.

"The vessel flees, but we note that they have managed to speed up twice," he said carefully. "*Sundering Wrath* has matched them, at present."

"Have they now?" she asked sharply.

"Each was somewhat random, so we cannot tell if they originally held back," he nodded. "Since then, I would have ordered my machinists to push the margins of safety, were I *Marrakesh*'s Captain. A man named Padraig Boru, but one we do not know much about."

"Damage to *Sundering Wrath*?" Divna pressed. "Either weapons or machines?"

She'd felt the keel shudder under that one hit. Extreme range for a heavy particle cannon, but wasn't that the whole point of the tests *Marrakesh* had been running?

Borsheva had found some new solution to the problem of power, throughput, containment, and accuracy.

A deadly improvement, at that.

"Armor absorbed most of the shot," Dragutin replied. "Three crew sent to medical, with one already returned to duty and the other two stable. None of our weapon systems suffered degradation, but *Marrakesh* has a greater range than *Sundering Wrath*, if they manage to elude us in real space. One twin turret mounted high, with what appears to be a full three hundred and sixty degrees of coverage. My officers postulate that the current design allows one hundred degrees of elevation, from minus twenty to plus eighty for engagement. The only blind spot appears to be directly under the tug, but they can easily roll in place if we attempt it."

"Best to stay horizontal, then?" she asked, testing the man.

"At least until our own heavy turrets range better," he nodded. "Then we should flare to broadside them, as the comparable weight of fire greatly favors us."

Divna nodded. Textbook, all the way across the board.

Marrakesh had a longer spear, but she had more arrows and better armor than a tug.

High-speed flight meant that they were farther away from support with every passing hour, though they might still try to circle back to Albany in Ghost-space and attempt to set an ambush. Each time they turned, though, *Sundering Wrath* had gained a little ground.

If they got close enough...

She wondered if they would try to return to Albany somehow, in Ghost-space. She would chase.

And at that point, she would see if the defenses at Albany were sufficient to thwart her.

The two sides were evenly matched with *Marrakesh* involved.

If she could isolate them, she could crush the smaller ship.

And they could not run at this speed forever.

What would they do next?

11

Chance reviewed her notes, eyes a little bleary and crossed from digging so deeply into Dr. Borsheva's—no, she insisted on Alexis—on Alexis's notes. Theory. Design. Military reviews.

A powerful improvement on the standard heavy particle cannons that cruisers mounted. Possibly also something that could be scaled up enough to mount on the big Ships-of-the-Line.

Assuming that *Marrakesh* could escape today.

"Would your Captain Boru really burn out the systems?" Alexis asked.

"If it keeps us alive and gets you home?" Chance asked. "Absolutely. What I can't tell you is if it would be enough."

"No?" Alexis pressed.

"We've only got the normal heavy twin turrets fore and aft for a tug," Chance nodded. "You've added a fifth and sixth barrel to that. A Leviathan has two turrets fore and aft, and those are all triples. Plus, they usually have a longer range than what we mount, though you actually have the longest. They're still able to fire twelve heavier barrels at us if they get to broadside. We have a lot of missiles to keep them honest, but that's a whole other set of maneuver equations, and we'd have to be slugging it out with them to bring that into play. Ugly. Just ugly."

"And we cannot win?" Alexis seemed despondent.

"Padraig has a good rep," Chance told her. "I might have been flying a desk for the last few years, but he was Gunner and then First Officer on *Nemesis* before this. That ship got into a number of tussles, though he doesn't like to talk about it much. I know because I looked him up from my staff job when sailing orders finally got approved."

"You wanted to return to space?" Alexis asked.

"I signed up to be a sailor, Alexis," Chance nodded, smiling. "Being a mom just meant that I had to stay closer to home for a few years, but Robin's got the tykes taken care of while I'm out fighting in the war."

"I see," Alexis nodded. "What should I be doing next?"

Chance stopped and considered everything the woman had brain-dumped over the last several hours. It stuck in her craw to run from a fight, but even Chance Messier was willing to admit that *Marrakesh* was badly outclassed by a Leviathan. Maybe if they'd mounted a pair of combat modules, or better, a pair of missile battery modules, they could have made it a fairer fight.

"They have armor on the bow and broadside," Chance mused aloud. "And we can estimate how much, based on various things. Could you calculate the absolute maximum range that one of your guns could penetrate that armor, for the next time we fight?"

"Certainly," Alexis nodded. "All the formulae are in my notes, so what I need is a calculator. Now, however, is one of those times when it would be nice to have access to hyper-intelligent systems that could do all that math for me, once I told it the problem."

Chance bristled but didn't let the woman see it. Smart systems were too dangerous. *A'Zedi* kept their computers dumb and functional, rather than pushing the envelope on what might make them a new life-form.

Wronlori didn't have any such qualms, but they had never faced the negative outcomes of handing over too much of their lives to computers. Or maybe they just didn't care. *Wronlori* was a much more communal society in many ways, so people weren't supposed to think for themselves.

You answered to senior officers and group leaders and let them think for you. At what point would a hyper-intelligent computer system see itself as superior to mere organics and take charge?

Chance nodded instead. Easier, but that also led you into cutting corners in thinking.

Or worse, not thinking, because some machine could do it for you instead.

No.

A'Zedi prized the human mind, rather than the electronic one.

In a few hours, they might be putting that to the test.

12

─────

Kaitlin studied her various teams. The young post-doc was technically Dr. Ryan Donal, but he resisted any title, which went over well both with his own technicians as well as her crew.

Right now, Ryan had a grease stain running cuff to elbow on his right arm, from sticking it inside something to make a manual adjustment.

Kaitlin drew him away, but kept the youngster on her own right, where she wouldn't brush against the grease.

"How quickly would you be comfortable with your new adjustments, if we got the order to rapid-fire?" she asked.

He was taller than her, but most people were. She probably out-massed him, as he was average in just about every way, from reddish dark skin to nearly black hair to skinny build.

The brains marked him as soon as he opened his mouth.

"The generators can run flat out on standby," Donal replied, eyes unfocused. Or focused on a point several million light-years away. "The batteries are new enough to take a lot of cycles. I think the capacitors will be the choke point at first, building up the charge to detonate the pellet properly, then focusing the magnetic bottle to aim it downrange. At some point, even the generators won't be putting out power fast enough, though, so that will slow us down."

"What if I had ship's power routed in?" Kaitlin asked, watching him.

Around them, a dozen or so folks nodded, murmured, and listened, but nobody else got involved.

Then she watched the young man pull a pad of paper and a pencil out of his pocket, quickly writing something in a crabbed hand that almost looked like hieroglyphics when she looked.

At that point, Donal turned to one of his folks and asked several questions so esoteric that Kaitlin didn't understand anything except the tone. A question, but the answer was tentative.

The verbal equivalent of a shrugged *"Maybe?"*

Donal wrote down several more lines, then mathed it all together, and looked up at her.

"Sometime around the twelfth shot, I think we'll need to draw on *Marrakesh*'s generators," he announced. "Since they are already connected, you'll need to let someone know that we'll be standing at the door, cup in hand for some sugar."

Kaitlin smiled and nodded. The young man was incredibly smart but hadn't internalized Padraig's consensus that those big guns overhead might be the single most important thing on the ship if that Leviathan caught them. Jareth Ahearn would happily feed them everything they needed to keep the guns firing as fast as they could.

"And the cooling systems?" she asked.

Donal shrugged in an endearing way.

"It was easier to take the plant off a decommissioned Ship-of-the-Line," he replied. "It's rated for a triple turret, but we only mounted a twin because of the extra monitors and sensors we needed. According to my calculations, as long as we have power, they will hold at least until something breaks, and I can't tell you what might go first."

"Good enough," she replied.

Kaitlin looked around the combined groups.

"We've done all the maintenance we can," she announced to the gathering, getting back nods. "Split into your normal teams, then half of you go on break immediately. Dinner then nap. In three hours, we'll switch. Then someone needs to make coffee thick enough to stand a knife upright, because we'll need it later. Questions?"

Turned out that Rock, Paper, Scissors was how the two sides decided. Kaitlin rolled her eyes and let them. Morale was high, though she'd been watching Borsheva's people. And had Den or one of his people with every single one of Donal's while they'd worked.

Ostensibly to learn the finer details, but most of her folks knew it pretty well by now.

She was watching for a saboteur.

13

―――――――

Padraig had checked the scans, but that Leviathan was still dead astern. As long as nothing happened to *Marrakesh*'s systems, they'd stay that way.

And if something did, they might drop into battle in a matter of seconds.

He had called Chance forward, then pulled her and Nyssa Taggart into his office, just off the bridge.

"What can you tell me about the nebula?" he asked the young Squire.

"As far as I can tell, nobody has ever done more than a quick scan from a distance, sir," Nyssa replied, hands clenching and unclenching like she wanted to be tapping controls to bring up screens filled with information.

He felt the same way.

"Nobody?" he asked, a little surprised.

The Survey Corps had that responsibility, but Albany itself was the back of beyond, then they'd gone a ways past that.

"There are some older notes," Nyssa nodded. "Not updated in nearly a century, though nebulae like this don't change very rapidly. If we simply maintain all our passive gear as we go in, we'll easily be able to overwrite the little currently known when we get back. If it matters."

"It matters to us right now," Chance broke in delicately. "Then we'll file it all later, with your name as principal surveyor."

"Me?" Nyssa asked. "Oh."

Padraig nodded. Young, but incredibly smart, and learning rapidly, both about herself as well as her job.

"Assuming the Leviathan wants to cut us off if we try to turn away, I need you to find our best entry point at high speed, Taggart," he told her. "And what we should expect Ghost-space to be like as we cross the outer boundary, since I'm not aware of anyone trying something like this. Well, and surviving. I'm sure there are many stories of smaller ships running from larger ones, trying to get lost in there."

"Aye, sir," Nyssa nodded. "To someone watching from the side, there should be a tremendous flare across the sky, like a comet nearly a light-hour long, assuming you were in the right place and watching with Aetherial Sensors. Same when the Leviathan enters the thicker parts chasing us."

"How quickly will that fade?" Chance asked.

Nyssa paused, automatically reaching for a keyboard before she caught herself.

"I think less than a minute, sir," Nyssa replied, trying to sound certain.

Padraig could hear the questions in her voice.

"Enough to track us?" he asked.

Nyssa shrugged.

"They'll be too close behind, sir," she finally said. "If anything, it might be something like a double rainbow to an outside viewer. When we drop out, they'll have to time it just right to end up close enough to shoot at us again. More likely is that they'll land long then have to double back and fire missiles. Assuming we stay put?"

"We'll know that when we get closer, Squire," he nodded and smiled. "My hope is that you can manage to track them using only passive sensors, rather than having to turn on any sort of targeting spotlight that will let them see us."

"The Survey module makes that possible, sir," Nyssa said, brightening up tremendously. "I've got capabilities equivalent to a fleet scout available. And it was designed to scan at solar system distances, so we should have an edge, assuming they aren't somehow equally prepared for this."

"Excellent work, Taggart," he said. "You get ready to go back on duty now, relieving Tameron. When we get there, all the sensor gear in the module will be under your command. Questions?"

"No, sir," she said.

"Dismissed."

She bounced up and smiled, retreating quickly and closing the hatch.

Chance studied him.

"What did you learn from Dr. Borsheva?" he asked his First Officer.

"That she prefers Alexis much of the time," Chance grinned. "I have had her calculate a number of engagement rings, based on the accuracy and firepower of her systems."

"And?"

"And we can hit from farther away with two barrels," Chance nodded. "They can hit back harder with a bigger twelve to our smaller six. What's a nebula going to do to particle cannon beams?"

Padraig smiled. It felt evil on his face.

"Mess them up about as bad as it will everyone's sensor equipment," he replied. "The extra hydrogen will absorb and diffuse beams severely, so all your range calculations will be off. But so will theirs. That's fine, because engaging them in a broadside slugging match is a dumb and fast way to die."

"Missiles?" Chance asked.

"They will have to be programmed to run to a set of coordinates, then separate into their component submunitions and target a cone," he said, turning serious. "Our job will be to either calculate where they are or find a way to lure them into a position where the missiles will be effective. We don't have all that many, being a Tactical Transport, so we'll have to make them count."

"What about the Leviathan?" Chance pressed. "I've looked them up while talking to Alexis, but we don't really know much about them in a situation like this."

"Agreed," Padraig nodded. "Normally, you'd have a squadron of them with escorts out front, like our battle line. Or maybe just all the gunboats as a massive, combined wolfpack. Out here, we have one advantage, because they risk us getting away if they launch and we immediately run. The problem will be detecting gunboats deployed before they fall on us and do enough damage to keep us put."

"But you have a plan," she said, not even a question. An observation.

"I do," Padraig replied.

She smiled when he told her what it was.

Now, he just had to figure out how to make it work.

14

Padraig settled into his station. Food and potty break had been taken care of already. Coffee in his favorite sippy cup, itself latched down against losing artificial gravity in battle, which happened far too often when titans began pounding on each other with sledge hammers.

Crews as rested as they could be, with many of them facing their first battle and learning how to handle the stress as they went.

Nervous smiles greeted him when he looked around, fading to the sorts of grim determination that did his soul good to see.

The *Sovereign Collective Directorate of A'Zedi* hadn't started this war. Or the previous several for that matter. *Wron-lori* was intent on conquering the galaxy, it seemed, and would not take no for an answer.

Until somebody made them.

Padraig would have been utterly shocked, though, a year ago, had he been told that he'd be in this position. And confident that he could at least get a tactical win out of the situation as he read it. Really, escaping when *Wronlori* had sent a Leviathan after him would be a victory.

He still wanted more. Damned bullies was what they were.

They had attacked Eworn without provocation. Without even bothering to send a declaration of war until several hours after their fleet had hit the system. It was not the first time that they had pulled that sort of stunt, either.

Culturally, the *United Technocracy of Wronlori* seemed to feel that apologizing for the message not arriving before the action would make it all better later.

Padraig wished he had his own capital ship today to teach them some manners.

Tomorrow, maybe.

Today, escape.

"Radio, time to insertion?" Padraig asked, looking at Nyssa Taggart.

A lot rode on her shoulders, but he had confidence in her as well. Strong shoulders, stronger than even she'd understood a week ago.

"Seven minutes, Captain," she replied crisply.

Food, coffee, nap. They did wonders.

"Distance to enemy warship?" he asked.

"Seventeen light-seconds and holding, sir," she said.

He keyed the channel aft.

"Engineering. Ahearn."

"I wanted to thank you personally, Knight Ahearn," Padraig said, perhaps a little louder so that everyone on the bridge as well as Ahearn's folks would hear it. "Your team opened an extra three seconds separation on them over the last several hours, in spite of everything they did to try to run us down. Nicely done."

He heard faint cheers in the background before he cut the

line. They needed to know how important they were, so often blind back in Engineering and occasionally taken for granted.

A new crew on an old, worn ship. Not how he'd wanted to bind them into a tighter whole, but he'd take it. They were all quickly becoming a team.

Padraig opened the most recent updates to the ship's log and reviewed them. Time, place, status. Details about everything up until now, to be appended onto the report he'd sent six hours ago.

Little new, except for his plans on how he intended to maneuver for the coming engagements. It would likely be over before anyone at Headquarters read this, but it would be committed to eternity at that point, for good or ill.

One Tactical Transport Cruiser against a *Wronlori* Leviathan. In single combat.

May the best captain win.

"Radio, seal and encrypt the latest log updates," he said, locking eyes with Nyssa as he spoke. "Then transmit it and stand by to cut all active sensor emissions."

"Sir?" she asked, eyes a little big again.

Next to her, Zarah Halloran glanced back as well.

"We'll be going in blind and inertial, people," he said simply. "Nyssa has scanned that margin and those depths better than anybody else ever has, and I'm willing to include our friends back there. We know what's coming. I don't want them somehow reading our own sensor echoes across the gap of Ghost-space and figuring out what we plan to do."

"Oh," Nyssa said, then turned sharply professional with a nod. "Encrypting now, sir. Transmission in...two and a half minutes."

Padraig nodded augustly, like one of those ancient gods

from pre-history, seated atop his throne looking down on the primitives below.

All a bunch of hooey, but it did let him convey calm certainty to his crew. They needed that. Ninety-day-wonders and *Three Days out of Uni* was something of a catch-phrase that described many of them.

And he himself was years ahead of his own schedule for a cruiser command, as he'd plotted it out twenty years ago.

But they were here, now. His crew. His people.

He would see them home safe.

"Message package transmitted, Captain," Nyssa spoke up, breaking the ominous silence that had descended on them.

"Separation still seventeen light-seconds, Squire?" he asked.

"Affirmative, sir."

"Cut all active transmissions, Radio," Padraig ordered. "I want us running as silent as we can."

"Aye, sir," Nyssa replied, clicking various controls on her board. "All systems transitioning to passive mode *now*, sir."

His board on the right side, echoing hers, took on the feel of an animated display. Best estimate calculations, when the computer didn't have as much information, and wasn't smart enough to think on its own. Better that way, anyway.

Padraig keyed open the channel to have his voice emerge in every chamber, including restrooms and freezers.

"All hands, stand by for battle," he said. "Helm, as you bear. Weapon Teams, unlock and prepare to open fire."

Padraig nodded and cut the line. Everyone not on one of the bridges would be blind to what was happening outside. There would be only sounds and fears to identify if something had gone wrong.

"Halloran, take us in."

15

BRIDGE, SUNDERING WRATH

Divna grimaced, but only Captain Maric was in a position to see it, as all the other stations faced outward against the bulkheads themselves.

"Repeat that?" she asked in a quiet voice.

"*Marrakesh* has just shut down all scanner activity," he said again.

"And how far out are they?" she pressed.

"Sensors," Maric raised his voice. "Time to the boundary of the nebula?"

"Ninety seconds and closing, sir," came the reply.

Maric turned back to her, awaiting...something. An outburst, perhaps.

"And we're still able to scan them?" she asked.

"Affirmative, Marshal Babic," he nodded.

Divna studied the plot on the forward wall of the bridge with a grimace, unable to fathom such behavior.

Then it became clear. She muttered a curse under her breath.

"Sir?" Captain Maric asked.

"They expect the nebula to blind us sufficiently to hide," she said.

Divna paused.

"Sensors," she raised her own voice. "Keep a hard lock on *Marrakesh* as long as possible."

Technically, Maric's order to give, but all he would do would be to repeat her words.

"Helm," Maric followed up. "Maintain current distance but be prepared for *Marrakesh* to drop out of Ghost-space and calculate your own exit to drop us as closely as possible. All weapons systems, stand by to open fire as soon as you have a target to engage."

Divna nodded.

They'd chased *Marrakesh* for most of a day, slowly closing the gap for a time before falling back some. Not enough that the *A'Zedi* ship could escape, but too far to engage with cannons.

In Ghost-space, one had to be almost on top of your foe to hit them. And if *Marrakesh* dropped out, they would vanish too quickly for even that.

Captain Maric turned to face her now.

"I have crews in the gunboats," he said. "Except for Number Two, which suffered sufficient damage in our first encounter that it needs to be repaired more than we can handle in the field. Should the other three prepare to deploy?"

Divna was torn. Nebula fighting like this was almost entirely a hypothetical training exercise done during officer candidate school. She wasn't aware of any battles fought in this sort of terrain in the current generation, if not earlier.

"How blind will we be?" she asked.

He was almost a decade younger, so that much closer to those same classes. Those same thoughts.

Maric grimaced.

"I won't know until we are in the midst of it," he admitted. "*Marrakesh* will get to pick the fighting ground, obviously, but in being dark, it expands our own cone of uncertainty. When we drop out, I will presume that we don't want to immediately turn on all of our own sensors, but instead watch passively so that we don't make ourselves a target for *A'Zedi* missiles coming out of the darkness."

"Agreed," Divna nodded. "We have better firepower, but if we launch, we run the risk of them immediately fleeing again, and forcing us to recover, since the gunboats do not have the Ghostdrives or consumables to get home with any speed. On the other hand, having three of them deployed allows us to scan that much larger of a volume, even passively."

It was her mission. Her decision.

"Hold off launching but keep the crews aboard and ready to launch immediately," she said. "If he remains in place longer than half an hour, he is probably going to hide until we find him or are forced to retire ourselves, as I have no doubts that Captain Boru has informed his High Command of the situation. Help is still several days away from saving *Marrakesh*, but we do not have that long ourselves."

Maric nodded. Already, things had gone sideways from the original plans, but no attack plan survives contact with the enemy. Hers had a number of contingencies, but chasing *Marrakesh* into an unmapped, star-forming nebula had not been one of them.

She would still make the best of it.

Divna turned back to the main screen and watched *Marrakesh* race closer and closer to the line that marked clouds of gas thick enough to be seen with the naked eye.

Star fog, with all that such a thing entailed.

16

Padraig listened with his ears as well as toes flat on the deck, but the transition to the nebula didn't cause any pings or ripples beyond what they already had running flat out in Ghost-space. One moment, theoretical open space, the next, a boundary of ionized gases spewed out by young, hyper-hot blue giants or being pulled in by collapsing whirlpools that would one day become stars themselves.

On his scan echo from Nyssa's boards, a freaking mess.

"Helm, down five," he ordered. "Starboard five and induce a slight roll. Random is fine, as long as we don't end up hitting anything big enough to matter in Ghost-space."

"Five, five, roll, aye," Zarah replied crisply. "Initiating."

Nyssa had added an animation to make things more obvious. A tremendous flare of cometary gases trailing out behind the ship on her boards as Padraig watched, like a god sitting above watching the chase come down to the deadly parts. It certainly looked pretty, but he assumed it was all special effects for folks to gaze at in wonder.

Behind them, a second comet appeared. The Leviathan, hard on their stern like a hungry shark.

Hopefully, that slight turn as *Marrakesh* entered would cause his foe to misalign themselves. Not that it would mean much, but when you were back in the sidereal world, it might mean the difference entirely.

"Radio, what's the distance to that one solar system now on our bow?" Padraig asked.

Nyssa paused and studied.

"One point seven light-years, sir," she said. "Estimated arrival time sixteen minutes at current pace."

"Helm, adjust yourself to bring us into the thickest part of the disk," he ordered. "Keep us roughly towards the inner edge of the habitable zone and plot a target to drop out of Ghost-drives. Solar winds will be thick there, but not dangerous enough to damage the hull in the time we'll be engaged."

"Aye, sir."

More of this stern chase. Two tadpoles racing through a thickening soup of proto-star material and the detritus of a previous generation whose celestial deaths had triggered the current round of star formation.

Padraig waited. That was the hardest part. He wanted to be pushing buttons and *doing* things. Flying. Shooting. Something. Anything.

Command was the loneliest job in the fleet because the decisions were his alone and he hadn't had time to train everyone to the standards they needed to respond automatically.

"Radio, status of the Leviathan?" he asked.

"Holding firm aft, sir," Nyssa replied. "Closing a little to make up for losing us slightly on the turn. Sixteen seconds will give them time to realign."

"As expected, Radio," he said.

He'd hoped that they might miss the deviation and overshoot, in which case he could turn and run like hell for Albany again, but that Leviathan was intent on herding him, so he had to be herded. Driven.

The ugliest parts would come later.

But still all too soon.

17

BRIDGE, SUNDERING WRATH

Divna watched the screen display a massive corona of energy in bright pink, where *Marrakesh* had entered the nebula. No doubt, there was something there, but she didn't know what it might really look like, were someone in a position to watch.

"*Marrakesh* maneuvering," the Pilot called from below and ahead, eyes intent on his boards. "Maintaining pursuit mode. Distance sixteen light-seconds and stable."

She looked over at Captain Maric. It was his chase for now. Her glory or reprobation later, but he would fight the ship.

"Sensors," he called with a nod back to her. "Keep a firm lock on *Marrakesh* and plot their location as closely as possible when they drop out. Pilot, that will be your target. Prepare to go dark when we drop out of FTL."

He paused and looked sidelong.

"We still assume he will attempt to hide, rather than racing through?" Maric asked in a murmur only she could hear.

"Both are options," she said. "Hiding gives him a chance, as I do not believe that he can escape our scanners otherwise."

Maric nodded with that.

"Offense units, stand by for engagement," Maric ordered. "Gunboats, maintain your readiness, but I do not expect you to launch immediately, so you may stand down to ready alert status."

Divna nodded. By the book.

Unfortunately, Captain Boru probably understood that book as well as she did. And was doing everything in his power to thwart her.

Whether he could, remained to be seen.

18

Padraig noted the time. And the estimated location, based on what Nyssa Taggart had been able to see from the edges of her Aetherials range.

Ugly, messy, and hot. All of that worked in his favor, as the Leviathan would have to make themselves a target if they dropped into real space with everything lit up. *Marrakesh* had three missile tubes down each flank, launching them horizontally.

Exit, orient, ignite. Hard burn at high acceleration ballistically to the designated location, then the warhead separated into component parts. Unguided at that point but moving at high speed.

"Armiger Nevin," he called, making sure his Weapons Officer was sharp. "What's the current load on your missiles?"

"Two of them are Three-point, sir," Maddox replied immediately. "The other four are Six-point, as are all the ready reloads. Launch pattern calls for the four Six-pointers first, followed by the two Threes, then Sixes in the tubes for a second salvo as needed."

"Excellent work, Nevin," Padraig replied.

No change, but Maddox was sharp today. On top of the details without having to pause and check his notes.

There would be no time to think if that Leviathan suddenly loomed out of the fog around them. Simply shoot and hope that a warhead broken down into high-speed submunitions had been fired true. Explosives weren't even relevant at these speeds because you had the hardened pie-slice of warhead moving as quickly as one percent of light speed when the engines reached burnout.

Padraig doubted that they would stand off and politely lob missiles at each other today.

No, this was going to be a knife fight in a dark alley.

At least he wasn't getting mugged in broad daylight in a parking lot, though.

That Leviathan was going to have to work for it.

"Helm, stand by to drop out of Ghost-space," Nyssa called, glancing over at Zarah next to her. "Ten seconds."

Padraig nodded.

He'd told Nyssa to take charge of things, and the young Squire was doing so. Waiting for him to relay an order to someone sitting right next to you, while it might look good on paper and in the regulations, had no place today.

"Standing by," Zarah replied.

Padraig took a deep breath and held it.

"Four, three, two, one, BREAK!" Nyssa counted down.

Marrakesh did lurch a little, but they'd been moving fast and just dropped into the mud. If anything, that could help because it might make that Leviathan overshoot.

"Out of Ghost-space," Zarah said. "Bringing rotary thrusters to zero now."

"Nevin, stand by," Padraig ordered unnecessarily.

Still, he needed everyone focused on their jobs.

"Radio, confirm that all emissions are shut down and we look like a hole in space," Padraig ordered.

"Affirmative, Captain," she looked up and made eye contact. "Everything is off, including transponders and navigational markers."

Padraig nodded. Every ship had marker lights, in case two ships had lost sensors and were relying on eyeballs to maneuver in close.

Nothing could be allowed to give away their position.

Until they fired every missile and cut loose with every particle cannon and maybe even the railgun pulsars, usually the last-ditch defense against inbound missiles, if you could hit them with enough energy to knock them off a collision course.

Marrakesh would probably look like a fire hose of bioluminescence, as thick as the solar wind and particle count were outside.

"Radio, time to intercept?" he asked.

"Four, three, two, one, mark," Nyssa counted. "Overflight achieved, assuming they marked us and got close. Passive sensors looking, sir."

Padraig nodded again. Nineteen, going on fifty, from the sound of her voice.

It would have been nice for a big splash to appear on her boards. Maddox Nevin would unleash hell without waiting.

Instead, things were constantly boiling and roiling around them. At purely optical wavelengths, it really was a fog out there, neon blue in places though punctuated by nearby stars. Tides swirled around them, driven by multiple solar winds competing with one another and heating up the mess until it was nearly one hundred degrees Kelvin out there.

Hot, by solar system standards. Still lethally cold.

"Anything?" he asked.

"Negative, sir," Nyssa replied, not looking up. "Too much noise around us."

He kept his face neutral when he really wanted to grimace.

It was exactly what he'd been aiming for when he fled this direction.

Now, he had to live with it.

19

BRIDGE, SUNDERING WRATH

Divna found the view hauntingly beautiful as they dropped back out of Ghost-space. In the same way that a venomous snake could be beautiful.

Blueish clouds around them, like a fog on a fall day, back on Paquete, her home world and the capital of the *United Technocracy* itself. *Sundering Wrath* was like an alligator slipping through the shallows in search of prey.

"Engines, all stop," Maric called as she watched and listened. "Let the ship coast on final settings, ready to accelerate again. Ride the gyroscopes to maintain course and heading. Sensors, maintain passive mode until ordered otherwise."

Assents, then the bridge fell silent.

The hiss of gases outside the hull was almost comparable to being at the top of an atmosphere, flying extremely low in orbit. The radiation around them was nearly blinding, but that was the result of several young, hot blue giants madly burning up all their gas on the way to another cycle of supernovae to cause more stars to collapse around them.

Marrakesh could be anywhere. Invisible. Right under their nose or several light-seconds away.

On a scanner board, everything looked tiny. And it was so much worse when you had to use passive scanners across a volume that might take a photon of light as long as four seconds to cross.

"And now," Divna announced, mostly to break the strain of silence before it turned into shackles, "the hunt commences. Everyone stay sharp, as they are close and can still bite us."

Heads nodded, facing away from her where she couldn't see expressions, save the way the shoulders rested. Or the way hands tapped keys.

"What do we know?" Divna asked Captain Maric in a quieter voice, letting the rest of the bridge crew work.

He tapped a few keys and brought up a localized map, as they'd scanned it right until the last moment before arrival.

Hopefully, they'd slid silently into the water, and the deer coming down to drink hadn't noticed them.

"*Marrakesh* specifically picked this ground," Maric replied. "We're close to a star that should be at the top of yellow, verging onto white, when it finally finishes collapsing in several million more years. Scanners show several places that will eventually form planets, but are currently only disks of matter coalescing. We will need to maintain a hard watch, as the ship had significant velocity relative to the cloud and there are rocks out there that might impact us. Otherwise, we are waiting to see if we can locate them, just as they are us."

"Keep your defensive crews hyperalert," Divna replied. "I'd rather you shot at ghosts than have *Marrakesh* sneak up on us and fire a missile spread that we are unable to engage until they are nearly upon us."

"Understood, Marshal," Captain Maric replied.

She watched him transmit various orders to his own crew, heads bobbing as they absorbed and refined.

Messy.

She almost hoped Captain Boru would run, just so she could escape the dread of fighting here.

Almost.

20

———

Kaitlin studied the crew that Dr. Borsheva had brought onto the ship with even greater intensity than she had following the maintenance cycle they'd done.

None of Borsheva's people had been left alone to do anything, but she couldn't help but worry that one of them was a spy. A traitor, moving like a worm inside the apple that was *Marrakesh* and the *Directorate*.

Padraig was certain that this mission had been leaked somewhere. That the Leviathan knew where to find them, and who they were looking for.

Heads would eventually roll, but she had to assume that someone, somewhere, had made the determination that assassinating or capturing Dr. Borsheva was worth burning a few spies in the process.

She just didn't like holding the wrong end of that stick.

Right now, she was on Deck Five, one level down from the turret itself, in a secondary control space where Borsheva and Ryan Donal had installed all manner of equipment to track the workings of their guns. Donal was having a conversation with one of the younger geniuses on the team, with three technicians standing around them, occasionally offering opinions and arguments.

From here, mostly a background murmur, but the emotions were more nerdy excitement than worry.

Deep-diving into esoterica, not that she'd ever done something like that.

Den came up from below, messier than normal with more grease on his leg and a grin.

And he casually carried an adjustment wrench with a multi-docked head in one hand. One hundred and forty centimeters of adjustment wrench.

It looked like an ancient warhammer in his hand. Den carried it like the kind of smaller claw hammer a carpenter might use professionally.

She drew him close with a nod.

"Dare I ask?" she said in a voice nobody else would hear.

"Ya never know when something might go wrong, boss," he grinned. "Gotta be ready to *adjust* it on the fly."

"Unless someone has a beam pistol and is threatening to shoot someone, we'll want them alive, Den," Kaitlin reminded the man quietly.

He got a grumpy look.

"Broken legs don't count," she offered as a consolation prize, watching the man brighten right back up. "Are all your people being so obvious?"

"Negative on that," Den nodded. "Most have little stuff, but I've let them know that the only time someone is alone around here involves going to take a crap."

Kaitlin nodded, then paused and reconsidered. Mostly generators on the bottom deck, with a few control systems and backup batteries. Twin turret accessible on Deck Six, stuck out an extra level from normal. Here on Five, it was control stations and boards, plus a compact kitchenette, one-room head, and a small break room with over/under bunks to crash in. The levels below her were mostly hardware. More batteries and capacitors. Serious coolant systems that were way more than two barrels needed, but would let them fire as long as *Marrakesh* could keep a power feed pouring energy in.

"You have an idea?" Den asked hopefully.

"Keep your folks loose," Kaitlin said. "And assign the damage control team here until we need them. I need to go over to B-module and look at something. You come with me."

Den nodded and fell in at her hip as she crossed the deck to the hatch.

Usually, you didn't open the connecting passageway that was standard on most modules. Less risk of life support failures, fires, or other trouble. Today, it saved her from walking down to Two and crossing there.

Especially since nobody could exit the paired modules to the main hull in order to cross over.

The two hatches were mated with an extended airlock just deep enough for one person to cross, but she opened both and stepped through.

Over here, Five was the top deck, with a vast array of deployable and adjustable sensors mounted above, but still below the level of the Twins firing flat.

Marrakesh had been shooting broadside at that asteroid when all hell originally broke loose yesterday, letting these sensors parallax with *Marrakesh*'s own systems. Barrels of information had been accumulated.

Kaitlin had heard someone complain at one point that it would take them more than a year to catalog it all, to which Donal had reminded them that such a volume gave them that many more university credits toward their degree. The bitching had gotten quieter, but not gone away.

She grinned as she entered the Survey control room. This was Donal's usual station, seated next to Borsheva while the lesser members of the team had actually fired the guns, or maintained all the power systems allowing it.

Not quite jury-rigged, but everything had still been rough over there, with power conduits like hawsers running hither and yon.

This was a standard Type 2 Survey Module. Exactly like a few dozen or hundred others scattered around the fleet.

Den had followed her. Otherwise, the room was empty, with a few folks crashed out below napping after working their asses off up until now. Some crew members might be having some tea or food.

Downtime, because even in the middle of a possible battle, you needed to maintain some level of watch rotation, lest everyone get exhausted at the same time and start making mistakes.

Kaitlin sat in Donal's seat and watched the board. Nyssa Taggart had locked everything down to her own control earlier, so that she had all this extra Survey power at her fingertips. Kaitlin wasn't about to mess with that, but she did check the airlock to A-module.

Still closed, though Ryan Donal would head over at some point, she presumed. Or not.

Den stood next to Borsheva's chair.

"What are we looking for?" he asked, still holding his warhammer, but far less confident about it now.

Den was a worker, not necessarily a thinker. He solved puzzle stacking games at galactic expert level but didn't really branch out beyond that. Which was why she was the Stevedore, and he was the Docker.

"Your comment about being alone in the head," Kaitlin replied.

"And?" Den pressed. "What kind of trouble are they going to get to, taking a crap?"

"What if someone has some sort of radio beacon?" Kaitlin asked. "Or even a short-range radio that the *Wronlori* ship might lock onto?"

"Uhm…" Den offered sagely.

Kaitlin checked the deck hatch going down, but it was closed as well. The two of them were alone.

She keyed the comm and dialed.

"Messier," Chance replied.

Kaitlin liked the Commander. An easy-going woman, most of the time, who understood that shit written in the manual didn't always work when you had a situation on your hands. And would look at Kaitlin with a smile and say, "Let me know when you have it fixed," rather than demanding complicated action plans written down ahead of time, like some of the officers Kaitlin had known in her career as an enlisted swabbie.

"How do we go about muffling a radio signal from inside the ship?" Kaitlin asked without preamble.

Again, Messier was a smart woman, too.

"That is a damned good question, Kaitlin," Chance said. "I'd ask Nyssa, but she's a little busy right this moment. Do we have a problem?"

"We have a moment of paranoia, Chance," Kaitlin replied honestly. "Going back to previous conversations. Den mentioned someone sitting alone in the head, and I wondered if they might take that moment to turn on a locator beacon. I'd kinda like to not have my ass shot off today."

"Same, woman," Chance laughed. "Let me talk to Alexis and see if she can offer some ideas. Will call you back."

Kaitlin nodded when the line went dead.

"Gonna look a little hinky, offering to go potty with someone," Den offered with a dry tone and a grin.

"What you sailors do in your free time..." she countered.

Den snorted.

Kaitlin found a spot on the far wall and let her mind wander. She turned to Den after a few seconds of deep thought.

"I need you to inventory hardware, Den," she said, back to being *The Boss* and responsible for all the lives trapped in these two modules.

"What do you need?" he asked, hefting his warhammer again.

"A portable scanner," she replied, turning to him. "Something that you can call whatever when someone asks. Fire detector. Maintenance probe. You figure that out. Quietly ask someone, either here or aft, how to detect a short-range transmitter, then see if you can build a detector for one. Got it?"

"On it," he nodded.

Kaitlin noted the other airlock hatch sliding open, so this conversation was over.

"Go," she said, sliding across to Borsheva's chair as Ryan Donal appeared, swapping places with Gilroy as the Docker nodded and slid around him.

"Is everything okay?" Donal asked as he slid into his station.

Like her, he studied the board but didn't touch.

Kaitlin wasn't sure they could actually do anything here without first opening a panel somewhere and getting inside to cut out Taggart's overrides. Nor did she care to, though she would assume malice the first time someone else did.

Obviously, she needed to assign someone here. Maybe herself, since she had her own temporary bunk down with the swabbies.

"Checking on how the system is holding up," she lied to the man. "If something goes wrong, it's more likely to be here than with the guns. At least at first."

"You think so?" Donal turned around to look at her in surprise. "I thought that all of this hardware was fairly standard. What we had to do over there was a nightmare of wiring and theory."

Kaitlin nodded.

"And if we do need it, we'll basically have to burn it out," she agreed. "Use up six months' worth of testing in twenty minutes. That's what battles are like. But until then, these sensors are far more critical. Doubly so, considering how much more powerful they are than what *Marrakesh* usually carries."

"That much?" he asked.

"That much," she agreed this time. "Fortunately, the bridge can run everything remotely, so mostly I need to keep folks handy to repair anything that goes wrong, or even threatens to. Immediately, instead of in five minutes."

There. Perfectly accurate. Utterly obscure. Completely bullshit.

"One of your people?" he asked, eyes narrowing.

"Someone already trained to fix this equipment," she nodded. "Your folks are good with your systems, but that's all over in A-module. I'll probably camp here for a while, just so nobody else has to get pulled off what Den and I have them assigned doing."

"Huh," he said quietly, nodding with dawning understanding.

Boffin. Intellectual type who appeared average in almost every way. Average height for a guy. Dark brown hair. Darker skin than *Wronlori* but normal for *A'Zedi*. Eyes a dark, dark hazel.

Brains off the chart, but not someone you would look at and expect to be anything special when walking down the corridor.

Kaitlin didn't let that distract her, as any of Borsheva's people might be a threat, either to her or the mission.

And since the good doctor wasn't coming back aboard this module anytime soon, that meant a threat here.

Someone breaking the guns reduced *Marrakesh*'s overall firepower, but even with them, the ship didn't stand much of a chance against a Leviathan.

Breaking the Survey equipment somehow, that was a different problem.

Kaitlin settled in and asked Ryan Donal the sorts of small talk questions that two relative strangers engaged in when first meeting at a party.

Just not the party she had hoped for.

21

———

Chance cut the line to Kaitlin and turned to Lead Expert Bex Magorian, the woman currently watch-sitting for Helm if something happened forward.

A tiny woman. Slight build and hardly more than one hundred and fifty-three centimeters tall. And a physical throwback who looked more like she should be wearing the uniform of the *Enlightened Tyranny of Traisa*. Pale skin. Freckles. Hair just darker than blonde in a color Chance had heard called strawberry. Bright blue eyes.

"I'm going to locate Alexis, Bex," Chance said. "Then bring her back here. You've got things until I come back."

Bex nodded and Chance locked her boards down.

Moving quickly, she headed down a deck to where Alexis was bunked for now, uncertain if the woman was awake or asleep, given the amount of time everyone had been on alert over the last day. Or where she might be, eating or something.

Fortunately, there were two security troopers standing outside the hatch when she approached.

She moved to the hatch and hit the chime. The hatch slid open quickly.

Alexis looked tired. Worn.

"You okay?" Chance asked automatically.

"Stressed," Alexis nodded. "Come in."

"Actually, I was planning to haul you back upstairs and put you in my office for a bit, if that's acceptable?" Chance asked.

"Certainly," Alexis said. "Do I need shoes?"

Chance looked down and realized the woman was wearing only socks.

"Deck's been cleaned lately," Chance smiled. "As long as those aren't your favorite socks."

"Not even remotely," Alexis smiled back.

The woman exited the cabin, and they headed back toward the stairs, guards in tow.

Back on the Secondary Bridge, she stood the two troopers outside her office, then ushered Alexis in and closed the hatch.

Chance moved quickly, getting them settled and opening a comm.

"Wardroom."

"This is the First Officer," Chance said. "Can you send a pot of coffee to my office with two mugs?"

"Be there in five, Commander."

Chance nodded. Alexis looked like she needed it.

"What's the latest catastrophe?" Alexis asked.

"Nothing immediate," Chance said. "Kaitlin had an interesting question, and Nyssa Taggart and all her people are swamped with other things right now, so I thought I might ask you."

"Okay?"

"Working on the assumption that an assassin can no longer

get to you, Kaitlin wondered about someone having a beacon of some sort that might let the Leviathan find us," Chance said. "Or a radio loud enough to get a location fix on. Ideas on how to locate such a thing ahead of time or how to jam it without giving ourselves away in the process?"

Alexis leaned back in her chair now and Chance watched the woman's eyes flicker back and forth rapidly.

"How bad is the nebula outside?" Alexis finally asked.

Chance brought up a scan echo from Nyssa and turned her screen around for Alexis to study.

"Scans more like pudding than vacuum," Chance said. "But that's all the ionizing radiation lighting things up on various wavelengths as electrons dance around every valence shell they can find. Space itself is still a vacuum, looking with Eyeball, Mark One. Radio is the range I think I'm most worried about."

"And you've got the standard equipment locked out?" Alexis asked.

Chance nodded.

"Kaitlin's idea, so I'll feel safe assuming she's got that covered," Chance replied. "Thinking portable, but also expecting that the nebula is as much a surprise to any bad person as it was to me."

It was Alexis's turn to nod.

"All the ionization will help, then," Alexis said. "Might be hard to punch a signal through that mess to any depth. Be like trying to transmit to a satellite from the ground, without taking into account radiation belts in orbit."

"How would you do it?" Chance asked.

Hell, she had an expert inventor on her hands. One of the best known in the fleet these days.

A legend.

A rap at the door distracted them. Chance keyed the hatch open for the steward delivering the juice of life and two travel mugs for it.

A navy runs on caffeine and vitriol, a former captain had told her early in her career. All these years later, Chance Messier *believed*.

They were alone quickly, and Alexis locked eyes with her across the desk.

"Option One: somebody uses a ship system to transmit," Alexis said, ticking things off on the desk with her free hand. "That's covered by Kaitlin. Two: I'm guessing someone might have brought something with them from home, perhaps expecting to be captured and wanting to be able to identify themselves quietly when that happened."

"Something obvious?" Chance asked, contemplating sending a team in to inspect everything, which would precipitate the confrontation, but at least do it on her terms and her timing.

And piss off a lot of innocent folks.

"I doubt it," Alexis shook her head. "Everything would have been shipped with us and come through various layers of security along the way, because we only carried our personal luggage. It would be small and easy to hide, possibly anywhere in the Gunnery module, instead of just in their footlocker."

Chance grimaced. So much for that idea.

"Three, someone might turn on a targeting system in the turret," Alexis said. "I'm not sure if those are able to be over-ridden from the bridge or not."

"Hold that thought," Chance said, dialing a number.

"Bridge, Nevin."

"Maddox, can you or Nyssa lock the targeting scanners in

module-A from your end?" Chance asked. "So that only you can turn them on?"

"Stand by," Maddox replied. "Nyssa is nodding and pushing buttons furiously on her board. Okay, they are fully locked down at present and only these two stations can bring them online. Is that wise?"

"Ask Captain Boru when you have a moment," Chance said, cutting the line and turning her attention to Alexis. "Okay, what else?"

"Building your own transmitter from boards and gear and whatever spare parts might be sitting around," Alexis said. "Because the guns are still somewhat experimental, we basically included a shipping crate's worth of spares and things we could jury-rig with, rather than having something burn out and force us back to base."

Chance nodded. She'd seen the room on Deck Three of that module, items stacked on shelves and locked down, labeled in an esoteric cant that only engineers and nerds would understand.

There would be any manner of things available to someone desperate enough.

"Okay, so assume that it can be done, and there's little we can do to stop it," Chance shrugged, down but not defeated. "Can we smother it?"

Alexis's face screwed up sideways for a moment.

"Normally, you do that by broadcasting something louder on the same channel," the boffin replied. "Isn't that exactly the wrong response here?"

Chance considered her response carefully. Then she rose and gestured Alexis to join her. They exited her office and headed towards the main hatch.

"Bex, you're still in charge here if Padraig has an issue," she ordered. "We'll be forward on the bridge."

She needed an expert on the topic.

Luckily, she had one.

22

Padraig raised an eyebrow when Chance tromped in, with Borsheva and her two new guards following.

"What's our status?" Chance asked as she came to rest.

"Running silent," Padraig replied. "Might have had a ping of the Leviathan dropping off of Ghostdrive. Might have been a stellar burp."

Chance nodded and moved close, practically dragging Borsheva with her.

Quickly, she ran down the list of things that Kaitlin had asked, then those she and Borsheva had expanded upon.

"So basically, that sets me up to ask Nyssa one question," Chance said, several minutes of explanation later as everyone split their attention between boards and story. "Squire, is there a way we can start slowly putting out some sort of jamming signal on various radio frequencies, starting at low power and randomly varying it?"

"You want to start generating an electronic fog now, before any such signal appears that we might need to mask on the fly?" Nyssa asked.

Padraig was intrigued. He'd chosen his death ground for the advantage that the nebula would give to a smaller ship with better sensors.

Nyssa turned to look at him.

"Captain, I think I can do something like that," she said. "It helps if I only have to keep it on the old-fashioned radio frequencies and not worry about Aetherial issues. Should I?"

"Won't that light us up for the Leviathan?" he asked, looking at the three women ringleaders.

"It was Commander Messier's idea to start quietly, then delicately dialing the power up, sir," Nyssa replied. "Boiling the frog slowly, if I can make that comparison. It would help if we moved around somewhat randomly in the process, so that the signal didn't always originate from a single spot."

"And risks us being seen by the Leviathan," he said. "Can you mask your signal well enough, Squire Taggart?"

Insane idea, but at the same time it might solve a problem he'd never even considered.

The inside spy.

"I believe so, sir," Nyssa replied, eyes and face firm.

"What about a transport pod?" Maddox Nevin suddenly asked.

Padraig turned to the young man.

"Related to broadcasting a signal to confuse the enemy warship, sir," he continued earnestly. "Is it worth possibly sacrificing one of the two shuttles, and having it also rigged to randomly broadcast a variable radio signal, so that it doesn't always come from one location?"

Nyssa turned to the man and stared. Maddox blushed, but he was generally considered the aggressive hothead of the younger officers.

The man did have a brain in there as well.

"How to we control it?" Nyssa asked.

"Dunno," Maddox shrugged. "Hoping you could tell me. Maybe a tight-beam laser, if it won't reflect too much off the hull? Or maybe just write a program to randomly belch on various channels? You're the brains here, Radio. I just shoot stuff."

Padraig appreciated the way the older, more mature officer deferred to the younger one. Maddox Nevin was an Armiger, while Nyssa and Zarah were both still Squires. But this was Nyssa's show, and she'd been holding that load on her shoulders well.

Nyssa's eyes found a spot on the wall over Padraig's shoulder. The rest of the bridge fell silent, eyes mostly down for now in case that damned Leviathan suddenly roared out of the fog attacking.

"So that's my spiel," Chance announced. "I'm headed aft again, but I needed to explain it all in person. Let me know how Alexis and I can assist."

Padraig nodded to the two women, then watched his folks start whispering.

Nyssa paused and started to ask a question, but Padraig interrupted her.

"You are in control of those systems, Radio," he reminded her. "Until Maddox has someone to shoot at, we're listening to you."

She nodded and gulped. Padraig smiled. They were coming together. Perhaps forged in a crucible, but becoming a team.

Just exactly at the moment he needed them the most.

23

PERSONAL QUARTERS, SUNDERING WRATH

Divna had retired, after more than eight hours standing next to Captain Maric and watching his crew work.

They had been in the nebula for nearly two hours now. *Marrakesh* had burrowed down in the tall grass and hidden itself well. Maric had gone ahead and launched three of the gunboats, each under strict orders of silence.

Each was out there, listening. Waiting. Preparing to go for the other ship's throat as soon as anything resolved itself.

She was having a late dinner, then would move to a ready room for a few hours of sleep before Captain Maric did the same.

He had a good crew. Expert. However, they'd spent nearly thirty hours on duty at this point, stretching watch rotations to the point that many of them needed sleep.

Even Divna planned to take a watch, letting Maric and his people get a little more rest.

The chime on her hatch rang. She rose and keyed it open.

Captain Maric.

She gestured him in and returned to her food.

Her suite had three rooms. A front space for working that was the largest, with a sleeping room barely larger than the bunk and a private bathroom. Her dinner was on her desk. Maric took the seat across from her.

"Status?" she asked around a mouthful of stew.

"As of eighty minutes in, no sign of *Marrakesh*," he nodded. "All four vessels are maintaining strict radio silence, as we don't yet know where they are, other than the ship has not gone back to Ghost-space and cannot accelerate without being seen. If *Marrakesh* is detected, the vessel making the identification is to attack immediately while calling the others to assist. We assume that *Marrakesh* would likely flee if it is not sufficiently damaged in the initial engagement. At that point, the gunboats are prepared to be abandoned here, at least for a short time, allowing *Sundering Wrath* to immediately move in pursuit."

"How long could we maintain such a chase?" Divna asked.

"At Fast FTL, we are a little more than a day's travel from Albany," Maric said. "As they did not have sufficient forces to resist us without *Marrakesh*, we presume that the local *A'Zedi* force commanders would not try to meet them halfway, so *Marrakesh* would have to make it all the way to Albany to be safe under station guns."

"At which point, we madly flee back here and pick up your gunboats, before slipping away," Divna noted. "Hoping that no *A'Zedi* fleet happened to be close enough to be vectored down to chase us in turn, especially when fuel might become a problem if they did?"

"Exactly, Marshal," he said. "We've calculated a number of scenarios, but right now nothing is even close to critical, save that *A'Zedi* help might arrive. With our own scanner systems largely shut down, they could be almost on top of us before we detected each other, though I do have my crews listening for outside signals approaching."

Divna wanted to scowl but kept her face neutral. The plan had been good. The execution had been solid. Every sailor understands the importance of luck, and *Marrakesh* had gotten a good run of it.

First, to detect *Sundering Wrath* soon enough to flee.

Second, to have this nebula on the path that they had fled.

Third, to be able to stay far enough ahead of *Sundering Wrath* that Captain Maric hadn't been able to fire on them in Ghost-space.

And fourth, to find a place to hide.

"It will be a game of patience now, Captain Maric," she reminded him. "We have as much as a day before anyone might arrive, though do not assume we are safe here. After I sleep, add me to the watch rotation to allow your senior officers more time to sleep. It hasn't been that long since I was a Captain that I've forgotten everything I once knew."

He nodded.

"Yes, sir," he said. "In that case, I will have you take over in four hours, and I will sleep then."

"Excellent, Captain Maric," she said. "We'll catch them yet."

He nodded and rose from the chair, recognizing the dismissal and quickly departing. Divna didn't have much of the stew left, so she finished it as she considered her operation.

Her odds.

Still in her favor, but that would change at some point.

Hopefully, she would recognize it when it did.

24

Nyssa felt like she had the entire mass of *Marrakesh*, that Leviathan, and several nearby proto-stars on her shoulders, Atlas-like.

She wondered if this was what command meant. She'd never intended to be an officer, just a poor kid without a lot of interest in getting a job in a factory doing the same thing for forty years.

The attack on Eworn had lit a fire in her soul, already piled high with kindling she hadn't even been aware was there, so she'd enlisted. Tests had confirmed what she'd already known and largely hidden as a kid.

Nyssa Louise Taggart was way smarter than most people had realized. She'd learned young that smart kids got picked on, so she'd hidden herself in the middle of the pack. Above average, but not standing out, at least according to records that had accidentally shown a spike when she'd realized how easy middle school could be, before dialing it back a notch.

The navy folks had tested her. Then put her into electronics school. Then tested her again.

At one point, the captain in charge of the school had called Nyssa into his office for a chat. She'd been certain that they were about to throw her out, when instead he'd started talking about officer candidate school, and how much more the military would prize her than those fools she'd been hiding from.

Nyssa had thrived. Been commissioned. Gotten assigned to *Marrakesh* with such high marks that she was the Radio Officer for the whole ship, in charge of folks her parents' age in some cases.

It was all kinda frightening, but Captain Boru had been there every time she'd had a question or a need.

He relied on her. Trusted her.

Heady stuff.

Everyone was relying on her today.

She studied the small screen in front of her. Not the main screen that was listening to all the ambient electronic crap flying around as stars yelled at each other or snored.

This one had an analysis of the noise. The Armiger's idea had crystallized something.

She looked up, realized that the captain was studying her.

Nyssa blushed.

Being allowed to be smart was weird. Uncomfortable.

And yet, nobody teased her anymore. If anything, they went out of their way to brag on her, which was even *weirder*.

Maybe she could earn that.

"Squire?" he prompted, still staring at her.

"It isn't random," she said, tapping the screen.

"What isn't?"

"The stuff out there," Nyssa continued, gesturing with one hand to encompass...well, everything. "I found a sort of pattern, once I plugged in some astronomical data, sir."

"Talk to me, Taggart," he said, eyes big and intense.

"There are about forty different kinds of signals floating around us right now, Captain," Nyssa explained, aware that everyone she could see had tilted their head towards her, at least a little. Listening. Wow. "I have a randomizer program written that will cycle through all of them, whatever burps, screeches, or howls are normally on the radio bands everyone uses. If we program the autopilot on a pod, it can also make noise. If we start with a few low signals that randomly change the power behind the signal up and down as well as the waveform, it should be feasible to make it impossible for any intelligible communications to be received by the Leviathan."

"Will they be able to triangulate on it?" Captain Boru asked next, having already apparently understood and processed everything she'd said.

More wow.

Maybe that was why he was the Captain.

"Can that Leviathan listen to the transmitter itself and find us, if they figure it out?"

"Maybe, sir," she said. "They'd have to realize what they were hearing and acted on it. That's why we'd want to deploy an automated pod, so the *Wronlori* ship has an even chance to be hunting it instead of us if that happens."

Then he nodded.

Nyssa watched him dial someone on his comm line.

"Flight Deck. Rafferty."

"Squire Taggart will be sending you a pair of programs, Air Boss," the Captain said in that calm, soothing, *command* voice he had. "One will be an autopilot flight plan, while the other handles scanners and communications. You'll load those aboard one of the transport pods, then prep it for automated operations. Which one would you rather lose if it gets blown up as a result?"

"*Flight of Fancy* is in worse shape, sir," the man down below replied as Nyssa listened. "Runt of the original litter that mostly went to cruisers with better political connections."

She watched Captain Boru smile at that and made a note of his facial expressions, his hands, even the way he sat. *Captain*.

"On my orders, then, Air Boss Rafferty, prep *Flight of Fancy* for what might be a Viking funeral," Captain said brightly.

"Aye, aye, sir!"

Then he cut the line and smiled at her.

"Good job, Taggart," he said.

For a moment, it was like a warm blanket descended on her instead of the whole mass of *Marrakesh*.

25

Padraig checked the time. Arrival plus three hundred and six minutes. Just over five hours hiding in this mess.

Nyssa and her people had been listening all that time. The Leviathan had disappeared off the Aetherial Sensors right after *Marrakesh*, and not reappeared, so they were out there somewhere.

Waiting.

Watching.

Hunting.

He supposed that it might be possible to make a break for it. Suddenly turn and run like hell for Albany.

Except that even then, if the Leviathan pursued, there might not be enough firepower at Albany station to defeat a Leviathan. Drive them off, sure, but that let them escape.

Padraig wasn't interested in letting those *Wronlori* sailors escape.

And was smart enough to realize that a Leviathan might be too big of a bite for *Marrakesh* to handle.

Still, he wanted to try, at least once.

He studied his bridge. Folks had cycled in and out, with everyone coming off duty at least once in order to nap and eat back in the wardroom.

Sure, they could eat again at their stations, but Padraig wanted them up and walking around. Seeing different things so they didn't squirrel in too hard on their duty and start making mistakes of focus.

Maddox Nevin had just returned from a break, relieving the crew member watch-sitting with a nod.

"Armiger, what's the status of our missiles?" Padraig asked.

"Still a pair of the Three-point for ship-killing, Captain," Maddox replied instantly. "And the others are Six-point for a better damage cone. All six reloads are Six-point as well, assuming that we would be needing to do a lot of damage to gunboats as well as the main ship."

Padraig nodded. No change from...call it yesterday at this point. Before the nebula, when they'd still been running as hot as the Ghostdrives could sustain.

"Can we lay a trap for the Leviathan?" Padraig asked.

So far, nobody had blundered into one another. A four-light-second sphere was still huge, when everyone was hiding electronically and visuals were a mess from all the plasma and gas around them.

"Aye, sir," Maddox nodded. "What kind?"

Smart. The young man assumed that his captain had an idea.

Padraig did, but it harked back to a night of heavy drinking on leave with several friends, when Padraig had been Weapons Officer on *Nemesis*.

Years later, the whole weekend was a bit hazy. Probably for the best, all things considered, as he couldn't be called upon to testify.

"Nyssa has launched a pod with an autopilot program, though it is riding gyroscopes and maneuvering thrusters," Padraig said. "How do we reprogram a missile to let us better control the flight?"

He watched the man think.

"The missiles are designed to launch cold, then orient themselves for flight on a path we program in, before lighting the engines and accelerating to terminal velocity and separation, Captain," Maddox replied. "We should be able to change the orientation delay from four seconds to something longer."

"Insufficient, Armiger," Padraig said. "It will still backtrack to *Marrakesh* once someone detects the missile in flight. I need a way to hurl it clear of the ship with extreme velocity, so that it is well away from us before it lights, and then burns in such a way that we are nowhere close to the path our Leviathan will follow to locate us."

More thought. Padraig had gotten this far, but not been able to come up with a catapulting mechanism.

Or would a catapult itself be enough?

"Nevin, how would you go about building a purely mechanical device with sufficient power to throw a missile?" he asked.

"Purely mechanical, sir?" Maddox clarified carefully.

"Something that will not show up on any of Taggart's sensors," Padraig nodded. "That rules out cutting the engine module off of a second missile or using one of the docking tugs, because they would have to light their own engines to push that much mass with any speed."

"Do we expect it to impact a target, sir?" Maddox asked, eyes suddenly cagey in a good way.

"We don't care what it hits, Nevin," Padraig replied. "What's your idea?"

"Mass is the issue, sir," Maddox said. "The warhead is just a huge lump of steel designed to separate into three, six, or nine pieces at maximum speed, because even a nuclear explosive would be rounding error for that much mass hitting anything at that speed."

"Go on," Padraig prompted.

"What if we removed the warhead from a missile, sir?" Maddox asked. "Maybe just cut it off entirely, or replace it with a hollow shell close enough in size that the flight characteristics are similar?"

"Acceleration will be excessive, if it doesn't have to push all that steel," Padraig noted.

"Super, experimental new weapon, Captain," Maddox grinned. "We're found a way to double the thrust on our old missiles somehow. That ought to frighten any *Wronlori* commander out of his wits. And the reduced mass means that we could use the normal launch catapult, plus program in a long delay on the orientation system before it lights."

"Add a screamer," Nyssa piped up, not looking up from her own boards, where she was playing an electronic symphony that only space whales might appreciate.

"A what?" Maddox asked before Padraig could get his mouth open.

"Some sort of pinger from a sensor," she clarified. "Equipment to broadcast a signal, plus a big battery so it's loud. You want them to see it, track it in flight, and race madly after the calculated origin point, assuming that we're there, right?"

"Gold star, both of you," Padraig beamed. "Write something up and tell the machine shop to implement it on one of their missiles, then confirm before loading it into a tube."

"Aye, sir," they both said in perfect harmony, then started typing even faster.

Padraig leaned back and studied the depths of space that were hiding him.

If it didn't work, he'd probably run like hell and hope that he'd at least scared that Leviathan enough to matter next time.

Still, he wanted at least one bite at them.

26

BRIDGE, SUNDERING WRATH

Divna had returned to the bridge, letting Captain Maric have an extra two hours of sleep and downtime. He had been on duty for thirty hours at this point, and she'd seen the exhaustion in his eyes.

She wasn't much better, but she'd eaten, slept, and felt almost ready to go. *Stealing reserves from tomorrow* was the old saying, but she needed them today, and *Sundering Wrath* still had a long sail home to get to base, so everyone would have a chance to recover afterwards.

Mistakes from being too bleary eyed was the risk today. She needed to address that. Standing a watch herself, instead of maintaining her august aloofness, helped. And it hadn't been that many years since she'd been the Captain of a vessel like this, before being promoted to Marshal.

"Sensors, any change to your readings?" Divna asked the woman currently on duty.

She didn't know many names, once you got down to the enlisted folks sitting watches with her, but the ship was running something like normal night right now, with about half of the main officers having downtime.

"Negative, Marshal Babic," the woman said. "Ugly mess of noise on all bands, but especially heavy on a lot of the radio wavelengths. We'd be having a difficult time communicating with the gunboats if everyone wasn't operating under radio silence."

Divna nodded.

It was like skinny dipping in a lake at night, wondering if that thing that had brushed your leg was a fish, a log, or *something else*. The danger could be thrilling, but she'd have just as well chased *Marrakesh* back to Albany and maybe gotten a few lucky shots that let her do enough damage to kill or capture Alexis Borsheva.

Anything to neutralize that woman. She was simply too dangerous to be allowed to keep designing new weapons for *A'Zedi*.

"Pilot, show me a navigational plot on the holographic display," Divna ordered next.

The sphere filled up, even going so far as to include the haze, presumably for verisimilitude. Messy.

One blue arrowhead showing *Sundering Wrath*. Three green arrowheads showing the gunboats. Each had launched using nothing but the navigational thrusters that allowed them to dock, so none were all that far away, if battle broke out.

Certainly in no proper escort position. Nor poised to fall upon a tug like *Marrakesh*, except where *Sundering Wrath* would be close enough to join the assault quickly when the gunboats swarmed.

If only they could find the damned ship.

Divna called up a file on her own board and reread what little was known about Captain Padraig Boru. It was pitifully thin. Already, her own notes about this chase had doubled the length, merely from her suppositions on how smart the man must be to have reacted that quickly.

Perhaps dangerous enough by himself to warrant being killed or captured?

Borsheva was a civilian. Either outcome was acceptable. Boru, as a commanding officer, would be treated with extreme care, were he to fall into her hands. *Wronlori* captains would face the same treatment, so everyone in uniform played nice, expecting that they would be traded home after a reasonable time period.

Even a war wasn't an excuse to act like barbarians.

No, better to annihilate *Marrakesh* and kill all hands ahead of time. That also happened in war, though not many people talked about it much.

And some people were too dangerous to let live.

Had Boru been promoted to that level, at least in her mind?

Divna reconsidered what she knew. What anyone had known.

Marrakesh was an older ship. The last of *A'Zedi's M-Class* cruiser hulls still in commission, as far as her spies had been able to determine when researching this mission. Boru had been promoted young, so he must be good enough to impress his own Marshals.

They had reacted quickly to the attack. Quicker than they should have, with what her notes listed as a raw crew on their first ever deployment together. Fled madly, staying ahead of *Sundering Wrath* in Ghost-space, when it should have been possible to overhaul them and get in a few shots to lame them.

She put that down to new engines, fresh from a full refurbishment. And perhaps good machinists.

Then he had found the nebula, and burrowed in.

Vanished.

Eight hours and nobody had stumbled across each other, but she knew he was in here somewhere, just as Boru would know that he was facing *Sundering Wrath*.

Worse, by now he might have assumed the gunboats were deployed. If he fled at this stage, *Sundering Wrath* would be lacking almost half of their overall firepower, should she chase him back to Albany.

Down three, she could not take that system's orbital defenses on her best day.

Did he know he could get away right now?

Everything suggested that he was smart.

What was he doing with his time?

Divna felt a shiver take hold.

Was it possible that Captain Boru was hunting them?

27

Padraig perked up when the comm under his right hand chimed.

"Captain here," he said.

"Missile Deck, sir," the response came from Valeria Tindal, his Gunner. "Got your bird ready to fly."

"Talk to me, Valeria," he said.

"Per Armiger Nevin, we built a new shell over the front, Captain," she said. "Squire Taggart gave us a doohickey to stuff inside, already programmed to run when the engines light. Ought to be annoying as hell to someone listening."

He smiled at his two officers, both forward with him again after their breaks and side missions to do things.

It felt like things were moving toward a crescendo, but not quite there yet. Soon, though.

"Pull one of the Sixes from the tubes, Gunner," Padraig ordered. "Load your new bird, then slot a Three in behind it for reload. If this works, I want to be able to take a heavy shot at a Leviathan that might be sailing blindly by, chasing an exhaust path backwards. That will give me three and three."

"Understood, sir," Valeria replied with a smile in her voice.

The waiting was the hardest part, always.

The uncertainty. The fear that something was about to appear out of the haze to take a bite at you.

Everyone was poised to unleash everything they had, but if he started trading punches with a Leviathan at point blank range, *Marrakesh* would be quickly destroyed.

Better to hit them with a rabbit punch to knock them down, then start kicking.

And even Padraig knew that he was letting the ambitious side of himself daydream. The smartest possible move would be running as soon as the missile got their attention, when he might gain thirty seconds of misdirection.

His Ghostdrives had already proven sufficient to get *Marrakesh* away once. Something might break next time, but that might also happen to the Leviathan.

War was as much a matter of luck as it was training, though good training left you prepared to exploit luck when you stumbled upon it.

He had two cards on the table right now, either of which might make the difference later.

And he still wanted that bite.

"Nevin, what's your programming for the missile?" Padraig asked.

"Mass is down just above half, from what the Gunner tells me, sir," Maddox replied. "It should be moving pretty damned quick when it clears the tube. Then it is set for eighteen minutes, twenty-one seconds of forward drift before it rotates on gyros and fires on a path to bring them back past our bow and high, about thirty degrees offset."

"Why the timing?" he asked.

Padraig had given orders, then gotten out of the way. Maddox Nevin, with Nyssa's help, had done the work.

"Randomness works in our favor, sir," he said. "Someone might have tried this, but only given it five minutes to drift. Or some other even number that they might presume when backtracking. I'm trying to stay at least one extra step ahead of their Weapons Officer."

Padraig nodded. Well-trained people, willing to push the envelope into *weird* when the situation warranted. And this one did, as he couldn't think of the last time someone had done anything like this outside of a training simulation. At least Command School had done something similar, assuming a fight in an asteroid field, but nothing this messy.

He'd already sent a note home suggesting they add it to the curriculum. When he escaped, he could add more details about how to do it.

A few minutes of overall silence passed. Everyone tended to speak in hushed voices, even though it wouldn't matter. Padraig had considered dialing the lights down ten percent, just to get people into the mood and mode of hiding but had refrained.

It was still tempting.

His comm chimed again.

"Boru."

"Tindal, sir," she replied. "The tube is loaded and hot. Reload is on the tray."

"Thank you, Gunner," Padraig said. "Put a Six on the tray after that one. If we have to reload and keep fighting, I want maximum chaos available downrange."

"On it, sir."

The line went cold. Padraig turned to Maddox Nevin.

"Weapons Officer, launch one missile," he ordered.

All of this would be on Padraig's head if something went wrong. His logs and notes would let everyone back home know how well his crew had handled things, even if he ended up being relieved of command.

"Firing one, sir," Maddox replied, pushing a button on his keyboard with a hint of theatrical flourish.

The hull rattled as the electric catapult aft thrust the missile out of the tube and into the hazy, blue mess around them. Nyssa had an optical view of the missile, slowly rotating like a bullet as it moved away.

Padraig watched, impatient for the thing to spin in place and fire its engines. Normally, that was four seconds after it cleared the hull.

Today, it would be twenty minutes.

He considered his coffee mug. Empty, so he sent a general signal aft for the wardroom to send up another carafe.

It was going to be a long night, whatever happened next.

28

Kaitlin wasn't mesmerized by the Survey board in front of her adjusting itself and displaying information seemingly at random, but she wasn't going to deny being utterly fascinated by it. Kept her focused. And, as she'd told Ryan Donal, someone needed to be here if anything went wrong, ready to fix it immediately.

Kaitlin was too old to want to wade into a scrum with a wrench, if it came to that. Let the youngsters handle those tasks.

Instead, she sat and watched. Food and coffee got delivered. Folks came by to spend fifteen minutes standing her watch for potty breaks.

Otherwise, precious little to break the long monotony.

The hatch to the weapons module opened and Donal entered. Again, she was struck by how amazingly average the man was. It was like someone had calculated the exact mean and median on any number of statistics, then assembled the guy to hit every one of them as closely as possible.

Dark brown hair. Skin the darkness of *A'Zedi*. Height right in the middle. Mass right in the middle. Build right in the middle.

Face regular but not particularly impressive for either beauty or ugliness.

The only thing the man had going for him seemed to be brains. He had that in spades.

Donal walked closer, his face verging over onto either anger or confusion. Or both, if you wanted to mix it into a mean of frustration.

She was familiar with that one, but that came of years as a Docker on various ships, when you had to solve some problem and none of the tools at hand matched.

He moved to the chair and sat. They waited.

Both hatches were currently closed up against impending battle. Both of them wore emergency suits in purple, with helmets on their hips, hanging from the lanyard against the need to bottle up quickly.

Donal turned to study her. She allowed it, eyes open and questioning, but no emotion on her face.

"Why hasn't Alexis come back?" he asked abruptly.

Took her a moment, but she'd kinda been expecting the question.

"I'm guessing Captain Boru has some task better suited for her over there," Kaitlin lied breezily, throwing in a helpless shrug she'd worked out over the years.

It got to be second nature, when dealing with civilians temporarily aboard a transport and lost. Navy folks made a lot of pretty good assumptions and had generally been trained to keep their opinions to themselves.

Donal had neither.

"What could be more important than the cannon?" he

demanded. Well, asked hard. Voice hadn't gone up, just the inflection.

"I'm guessing at this point that we don't want to do anything to the turret that might mess it up," Kaitlin said. That much was honest. "So she can be doing other things, maybe related to the nebula. Meanwhile, if anything breaks, everyone else needs to be ready to fix it, including you telling them what to do."

All a level of horseshit, but a believable one. Not that she didn't trust the boy, but she didn't trust anyone right now. She could apologize later.

Everybody aboard this ship, civilian or navy, had passed the sorts of security backgrounds that allowed them to be involved with this sort of weapons research. And somebody had leaked. Here or back home, there was a worm that needed to be found before it ate the whole damned apple.

Donal seemed mollified by that. At least for now.

Everyone handled stress differently. Navy people were marked by the ability to sit and wait until they needed to explode into action. Civilians might not be so used to nothing happening for long stretches of time.

"What about you?" Kaitlin asked, mostly to deflect him onto some other topic, so that the boy wasn't going to just sit there and stew. "What's your expertise here?"

It was always useful to find the thing that someone wanted to nerd out about, then get them to talking.

Donal scowled at the universe for a moment, then his face cleared.

"I'm doing advanced research under Dr. Borsheva," he replied. "Finished my PhD in particle physics and mechanical engineering, but this project is the one that gets me set up to have my own research team."

"Nifty," Kaitlin said. And it was. "What do you want to build?"

Every mechanic had a dream. All of them. Everywhere. Total nerds, once you scratched the surface enough.

Donal turned a confused face towards her.

"If you had all the budget, time, and freedom in the world, what would you deliver?" she clarified. Or prodded. Something.

"There ought to be a thing beyond the heavy particle cannons that everybody uses," he said finally.

"Bigger guns or different physics?" Kaitlin asked, a little intrigued.

"A little of both," the young man nodded. "Instead of bottling up a stream of energized particles into a laser, find a way of making the beam act more like pure light, so that it can travel like a wave, then heterodyne back into particles on arrival. Greater range and power, once I solve some of the hairier equations."

"Under Borsheva?" Kaitlin asked.

Sounded revolutionary, but she also remembered being that age and thinking she'd solved all the world's troubles, if folks would just listen to her.

Later, she'd learned better what the limitations of budget and physics imposed.

Still...

Donal shook his head angrily.

"She doesn't think it will work," Donal replied. "At least not without a tremendously larger amount of power behind it, such that you'd have to have a station of dedicated generators pushing."

"Useful as a defensive system, then," Kaitlin pointed out.

"Especially if you can keep someone farther away from planetary orbit or wherever you are. What's the Navy say?"

Donal's grimace was back, but he smothered it and shrugged.

"Right now, they don't have that large of an experimental budget," he said. "I need to prove up these guns, then get my own team and have several smaller successes while I work on the mathematics in my spare time."

Kaitlin nodded.

Navies were, by definition, conservative. Sometimes to a fault.

Everything had to withstand the vacuum of space. Ships were expected to shoot at each other, gouging channels and punching holes in each other's armor. Everyday wear and tear of the rotary thrusters and Ghostdrives.

It had to protect the people aboard.

That meant that they tended to move in small increments and only after a lot of testing and confirmation. Helped that everybody else was the same way, though *Wronlori* tended to get a little crazier. But they had a smaller population base and a cultural fixation with advanced automation that let them try crazy things from time to time.

"How long will that probably take?" Kaitlin asked, mostly to keep him talking.

Boy sounded like he wanted to stew, and she'd stumbled into a sore spot accidentally.

"Years," he said disgustedly.

Kaitlin couldn't help but chuckle.

Donal's head came around.

"Dr. Donal, I'm fifty-two," she said. "At your age, everything looks like it will take forever, but a few years from now it won't be that bad. Especially not if you end up utterly revolutionizing weapons technology. You'll be at this for at least fifty years, if I had to guess, before you retire. Or some kid coming along who moves the revolution another step farther than you want to chase it. You've got time."

"Oh," Donal said after a pause.

Like he'd never really stopped to consider that part.

Kids these days, even when she'd been one of those hotheaded Turks in her youth.

"In fact," Kaitlin offered, mostly to derail him before he got to stewing again. "Right now, nobody is doing anything at all, at least until something happens. You might consider taking a few hours and working on your math. Navy and Borsheva are paying you for the time. Might as well take advantage of them."

His eyes lit up.

"Yes," he said suddenly, standing and heading to the interior hatch that would take him down to bunks below.

He didn't even say goodbye, but she was okay with that. The kid was wound a little too tight, and short of getting him drunk, she wasn't sure what might loosen him up. Now was not the time.

There was trouble outside. And maybe trouble inside.

She had to remain alert.

29

———

Padraig watched the countdown clock get close. Last minute of delay before ignition.

He dialed a number to open a smaller intercom.

"Weapons teams, stand by for our missile to light," he said, talking to the various turrets scattered around the hull, both offensive and defensive. And to let the folks manning the railgun pulsars and missile decks know that all hell might break out shortly.

Everyone had been on high alert for a long time, often napping in the turret itself to save the dozen steps to a comfortable bed. The next twenty minutes might be critical.

And they might be nothing at all, if the missile ended up facing a direction that didn't include any enemy warships.

Space was huge and the fog outside was chewy, at least by solar standards.

Padraig dialed a second number.

"Engineering. Ahearn."

"Just confirming that you have the Ghostdrives ready if we're running like hell again," Padraig said.

"Been standing here with one hand on the rocker's cover, sir," Ahearn laughed. "Say the word and we're gone."

"Not yet, Jareth," Padraig laughed with him. "I want to at least fire a shot or missile in anger at them here. Running with my tail between my legs grates badly on my temper."

"Understood, sir," Ahearn replied. "Me and the boys are the same way. Give 'em hell."

"Will do," Padraig said, cutting the line.

He turned to Maddox and Nyssa next.

"All set?" he asked.

"Expected flight path calculated, sir," Nyssa nodded. "I have all my passive sensors turned up to watch for eddies in the fog as well as radio signals from ships or spies."

Padraig nodded.

"Nevin, we'll open with particle cannon if anything happens," he continued. "I still want you to calculate a spread for your missiles and be ready to fire. This is a Leviathan, so we might also have up to four gunboats to engage. The Sixes are for the little ones, but I'll want Threes if we see the beast."

"Understood, Captain," Maddox nodded.

Padraig leaned back and considered.

He was likely only going to get one shot at this. If it failed to attract that *Wronlori* ship, he'd probably trust Ahearn to get them gone and home.

Or they might be shortly fighting for their lives, if the Leviathan happened to sail a path that put them right on top of *Marrakesh*.

Anything could happen.

Shortly.

Padraig watched the timer come down to zero.

30

It did not tumble through space. Internal gyroscopes in three dimensions spun with extreme velocity to hold the missile steady.

It flew through space like an arrow instead, lofted as one from ancient brigand vigilante who knew not where it would land.

Space was warmer than normal in the immediate vicinity, but not enough to affect its systems. Nor would the particle density per cubic meter greatly affect the casing as the missile moved at high speed, save to polish off the metal and paint of the nosecone at several times the usual rate.

It would ignite and accelerate. It would fly for a time, then achieve burnout when the engines exhausted their fuel.

There would be no secondary separation of warheads into independent missiles, as that hardware had been removed. Instead, it had a short-range radio transmitter designed to act like a siren in space, dopplering up and then down the range as it punched a clean hole through the bluish clouds.

Internally, a timer reached zero.

Secondary programming came online, telling the missile to locate six nearby stars and use them to triangulate itself against the original course programmed.

Off by seven percent. If the machine could think, it might have been impressed that solar wind and differential heating had not caused a greater tidal shift, given that the hardware had been drifting far longer than normally intended.

It made adjustments to the gyroscopes, drawing the nose down and to the left as the whole rotated to a new alignment.

Those six stars now appeared in a different spot on internal configurations. The machine confirmed things a third time and pronounced the results acceptable.

Had it sentience, it might have smiled.

Tertiary programming now. The motors lit, a solid fuel designed to burn from a central borehole outward, providing a stable thrust in an outward ring, assuming the fuel itself was within standard expectations of consistency.

A spark at the end caused an igniter circuit to blow a ring of flame outwards, combined with an electrical shock. Stable missiles would not merely ignite from heat. Safety was paramount, even in weapons of destruction.

The dual system caught, and the fuel began to oxidize at incredibly high speeds, generating thrust.

The missile itself had floated on a vector from the launching vessel. Not large, but sufficient that the targeting systems had to offset that with a burn.

The missile would continue to drift, even as it accelerated. It was not a perfectionist required to come to rest before firing in a straight line.

It was a weapon. Mindless, save for the programming intended to hurl it with great force into and through anything smaller than a moon when it hit terminal velocity.

Engines pushed, bringing it to relative rest, then sending it to one side.

The nosecone was light. The gyroscopes had been adjusted to take that into account, as the engines had already doubled the usual acceleration. Inside, a device began emitting a signal on several radio frequencies and wavelengths known to be commonly used as channels for organic communication.

It was not trying to talk to anyone, save to draw their eye.

The chances of the missile impacting anything designated as its enemy today were so small as to give meaning to *astronomical* in scope.

It burned fuel.

The clouds parted.

The missile announced itself to the cosmos.

31

BRIDGE, SUNDERING WRATH

Divna was at the tail end of her watch. Not to the edge of exhaustion she'd previously known but looking forward to perhaps a snack and some time to meditate if nothing else.

"Sensors," a voice rang out. Male. Excited. "I have contact!"

All the tiredness sloughed off her back like a falling cloak as the surge of adrenaline nearly lifted her off the deck.

"Track it!" she ordered unnecessarily. "Alert the captain and all primary officers currently off duty. Gun stations, stand by to engage!"

Everyone stirred, after sitting for so long and unable to do much of anything while they waited.

An alert siren blipped three times then stopped.

"Sensors, what do you have?" Divna asked.

"Missile track, sir," he replied. "But..."

She went cold for reasons she could not have explained.

"But?" she demanded after the man fell silent.

"Sir, the acceleration is frankly impossible," he said.

"Are we at risk?" she called.

That was all she really cared about right now. Weapons systems ready to engage, to claw at an incoming missile and hope to deflect it some by converting mass to plasma and using physics to push it off-line.

Sometimes, it even worked.

"Negative risk, Marshal," he said. "Track is down and away, moving at impossible speeds."

She wanted to ask what impossible meant, but the bridge hatch beside her opened and several people poured through at a dead run, including Dragutin Maric.

Divna nodded to the man as he slid in next to her.

"Status?" he asked.

"Someone fired a missile," she said. "Sensors Officer is backtracking it now."

"Taking command!" he yelled over the hubbub as folks displaced junior crew.

Divna stepped back, but called one order as she did.

"Sensors, plot the missile track on the main board and find me the launching platform," she said.

"Working," the man replied.

The main screen at the front of the room flipped from an optical view to a top-down solar one.

How fast was that damned thing accelerating? The vector plot finally got her attention. Most missiles never got to that speed. And this one was *still* accelerating?

What the hell?

Maric saw it, too. He turned to her with pure shock in his eyes for a moment, then reverted to professionalism.

"Pilot, plot a series of backwards tracks to intercept but do not engage your rotary thrusters," he ordered. "Weapons, take that line and prepare to fire. Again, hold until ordered."

Divna took a moment, then understood. He assumed it was a trap of some sort.

Why else fire a missile in all this mess, without first turning on all your sensors to lock onto the target? That someone hadn't done so suggested that they didn't know where *Sundering Wrath* was.

Trying to get them to spook?

"Sensors, do you have the plot?" Maric asked.

"I think so, sir," the man replied. "Hard to be certain."

Divna would grant him that one. None of this had followed the usual path, so a hint of confusion here would actually work to keep everyone honest. Worse than blindly charging in with the certainty that you have found your hidden foe.

Boru was probably counting on that.

"Show me," Maric ordered.

The plot of the missile showed the power with which it was moving. And a signal that almost seemed intended to draw the eye.

"Is that a targeting scanner of some sort?" she asked quietly. "Painting everything nearby and sending a signal with anything it sees back to *Marrakesh*?"

Maric paused in thought.

"Sensors, show me the signal that missile is transmitting," he ordered.

The waveform didn't make any sense to Divna. Nor, apparently, to anyone else on the bridge.

Divna was still concerned. Alexis Borsheva was aboard. What might that woman have come up with, given more than a day to prepare a surprise?

"Sir, Gunboat Two just turned on their targeting systems,"

the Communications Officer called from her corner. She sounded frantic. "Orders?"

Divna was close enough to read Maric's lips at the profanity he mouthed silently.

She commiserated. That ship had just made itself a target, but Divna didn't think it had found *Marrakesh*, or it would be transmitting coordinates and firing.

Nothing.

"Maintain silence," Maric ordered. "Maintain passive scans to see if that fool did anything useful."

He turned to her, and she saw how angry the man was. Someone aboard that gunboat had just ended his career, assuming he survived this battle.

She'd have seen to it herself, but Dragutin Maric looked like a man about to make an example of someone.

She approved of that, as well.

"No sensor echoes, sir," Communications called after a few moments. "Gunboat Two has gone back to silent mode."

Divna nodded. The damage had been done. Captain Boru would know that *Sundering Wrath* had deployed the gunboats. He could flee now and *Sundering Wrath* either had to give up, or risk facing Albany's combined forces without half of *Wrath*'s firepower.

They waited. Nothing happened.

"Sensors, are you monitoring Aetherial channels?" she asked, as the bridge had fallen into the silence of a tomb, broken only by the quiet purr of circulating fans.

"Affirmative, Marshal," the man replied. "No indication that *Marrakesh* has engaged Ghostdrives."

"That makes no sense," Maric rumbled beside her, again too quiet for anyone else to hear.

Divna considered remaining silent but moved to lean against the slightly taller man instead, so that she could speak directly into his ear without anyone else hearing.

"I think that *Marrakesh* wants to hunt *Sundering Wrath*," she murmured.

Maric recoiled away from her as if she'd slapped him.

"That's insane," he whispered back.

From across the room, it might look like they were dancing. Or kissing. Neither could be further from the truth.

"All he has to do right now is leave," she reminded the man. "What would you do?"

Maric's intense grimace spoke volumes, none of them pleasant.

"Are we trapped?" he asked.

Divna looked at him with confusion, then understanding dawned and the chill returned, a cold hand across her neck.

Sundering Wrath would have to transmit a signal to the gunboats to recall them. Since they only knew where the one fool was, it would have to be a broadcast, rather than a narrow beam like a communications laser.

Marrakesh would probably be able to pick it up as well. Boru would know where she was and hadn't fled.

Was he waiting for that signal, so he knew where to salvo his missiles? He wasn't close enough to truly surprise them, but everyone was at rest, so missiles were more likely to hit. Defensive turrets and railgun pulsars would engage as soon as they detected something, but would it be too little, too late?

Had they trapped themselves?

Knowing where a gunboat was limited the engagement sphere of where *Marrakesh* needed to look for *Sundering Wrath*. Was he already plotting a missile solution that would see the skies filled with fragments of steel hurled at them at lethal speeds?

All that came in a flash of insight that she needed to record for the records on Captain Padraig Boru. Someone had greatly underestimated the man.

Hopefully, she wasn't about to pay the price for that.

"Perhaps," she offered to Maric, poised as if dancing still. "Do we activate all sensors and hope that we can identify *Marrakesh* in time to open fire?"

"The parameters of that question make it impossible to judge," Maric replied. "We either do, or do not."

"I will leave that decision in your hands, Captain," she said. "We will set a timer, however, against which it becomes necessary to risk recovering the gunboats and fleeing back to *Wronlori* space, if *A'Zedi* has forces close enough to rescue *Marrakesh*."

"How long?" he asked.

"Six hours," Divna said.

There was no right answer because nobody knew if or when reinforcements might arrive. Framing the back end meant that things could be bookended so that Maric and his command crew could prepare for whatever chaos would likely erupt when the recall signal was sent.

It might even be necessary to order the gunboats to flee the nebula to be recovered later. They had short-range Ghostdrives for that sort of thing. Slow as well, but it would get everyone to safety outside.

If Boru chose to give chase at that point, *Sundering Wrath* would see them coming on the Aetherial scanners and be prepared to receive that charge.

How the hell had Boru managed to turn the tables so badly

on them that *Sundering Wrath* seemed to be at risk? From a tug?

Impossible.

And yet...

"Six hours," Maric acknowledged.

She watched him set a timer on his own board and nodded.

What the hell would happen next?

32

Padraig sat poised. It was hard forcing his shoulder blades to stay in touch with the seat back, so he had to concentrate on it.

"Nyssa," he said quietly as the missile fired. "Status?"

"Oh, shit!" she replied, nearly causing him to leap out of his seat. "Sorry, sir. We have a positive scan signal. A *Wronlori* gunboat just activated their targeting systems."

"And?" he asked, up a minor third from where his voice normally rested.

"They are tracking the missile, sir," she nodded. "The scan cone is pointed lateral to us, attempting to backtrack the missile's launch point without being anywhere close to *Marrakesh*. And they just shut it down again."

Padraig nodded.

Somebody had fucked up. It happened. Probably career-ending, depending on how charitable the Captain over there was feeling when all this was done.

"Back to darkness, sir," Nyssa said a few moments later.

Padraig watched everyone else relax a notch as well. Nothing like that to squeeze the bladder an extra bit. He'd taken the time to attach the suit's plumbing against that need but could hold it for now.

"Any hostile signals detected?" Padraig asked.

"Negative, sir," she replied. "Just the one, for two seconds."

"Good enough, though," he said.

Padraig dialed a number on his board.

"Secondary Bridge. Messier."

"Chance, you and Alexis take Nyssa's scan plot and tell me where our Leviathan is," he ordered. "She's going to be busy looking for more of them."

"Got it, Padraig," Chance replied. "What do we know?"

"Gunboat's location, relative to us," he said. "Everything else will be supposition on your part, until someone makes another mistake over there."

"We not going immediately to flight, since they deployed gunboats?" Chance asked.

"Depends on your sphere of uncertainty, First Officer," he replied. "I can still run if I have to, but being chased by those ijits has already pissed me off, so I'd like to maybe take a shot at them before I go. We can always put a Six, or even a Nine, on that gunboat's coordinates, then jump to Ghost-space. I'd like a kill today."

"We're on it, Captain."

Chance cut the line. Padraig turned to Maddox.

"In fact, have Tindal pull one of her Sixes for a Nine right now," he told the man. "A gunboat doesn't have the armor or integrity to survive even a ninth of a warhead impact, so we might get lucky, especially since they were so helpful as to tell us where they were."

"Understood, sir," Maddox replied.

Padraig leaned back again and watched the echo of Nyssa's boards. That missile hadn't gotten the Leviathan to reveal themselves for a salvo, but it had gotten a zone nailed down, if the gunboats were doing the same coasting from launch that the missile had.

And he was certain that someone lighting their rotary thrusters would have gotten Nyssa's attention.

How badly did he want this?

33

Chance cut the line and turned to Alexis. She'd taken up a spare station next to Bex and basically lived up here with them. Safer than being with her own people, at least until something happened one way or the other.

Alexis looked almost scared.

"I don't know anything about *Wronlori* gunboats," she admitted.

Chance nodded and brought up a schematic.

"Five-person crew," Chance explained, touching things on the panel. "Commander, pilot, navigator, engineer, and gunner. One turret overhead with a twin particle cannon comparable to what we use as a defensive weapon against them. Two missiles on external hardpoints. Short range and slow FTL capabilities, with a usual maximum expected deployment of seventy-two hours."

"Gravity?" Alexis asked.

"None," Chance replied. "Everyone is usually in semi-armored suits against damage immediately dragging them out a blown hatch, but they keep helmet faceshields open most of the time to keep their bottles from running empty."

"That looks like an eggshell," Alexis noted.

"They really are," Chance nodded. "The expectation in battle is four of them supporting each other as everyone closes, forcing you to either engage the wolfpack or the carrier, or splitting your fire and maybe not doing enough damage to force anybody back."

"What do you normally do?" Alexis asked.

"Normally, we run like hell when that much firepower shows up," Chance laughed. "Padraig is serious about us hurting someone first though, so we need to find them."

Alexis nodded.

"Okay, bring me up a navigation plot," she said.

Bex did so, with Chance watching. Might as well use all those brains.

"We know that they were drifting on launch," Chance said. "Bex, give me their best thruster speed, then bump it up five percent and reduce the entire sphere to that size. Our Leviathan is in there somewhere."

The board suddenly reduced significantly. Not enough to just flood it with missiles, as it was still more than a light-second across, but that made things way easier.

"Did we see them long enough to get a vector?" Alexis asked.

"Stand by," Chance replied.

She studied the data at hand. The direction of the bow of the ship, where the ping had emerged from.

"I'm going to assume that they were facing bow outwards from launch," Chance said. "Ready to go to full speed if they saw something, with an expectation that the others would rotate inward and come to help."

Alexis looked at her for a moment of confusion.

"Why?" the woman asked.

"Aggression is a trait selected for with gunboat crews," Chance nodded. "You want the crazy ones flying something that a single hit can destroy."

"Oh."

"Bex, do we think this is his bow facing?" Chance asked.

Bex shrugged, then added a cone of uncertainty in bright pink ahead of the vessel.

Chance flipped that cone around and moved it aftwards instead.

Suddenly, things were a lot more compact than they had been.

"The enemy warship will be in the back half of that," Alexis said. "As you said, aggression, so let's assume they have gotten as far away as they can on thrusters and are still coasting, if not using their maneuvering jets."

Bex added a conic cutout that eliminated the top of that cone, changing the remaining bottom purple now.

It might be worth firing a salvo of Nines into that zone. The odds of a hit were low, but it was a tiny volume, and you could play proportions.

She dialed a number on her comm.

"Boru."

"Padraig, Bex is about to send you a map," Chance said, nodding to the woman. "We think that there is a pretty good probability that a Leviathan is hiding in that space, but we're working on nothing but bullshit and physics."

"Understood, Chance," he replied. "Okay, got it. Excellent work."

He cut the line from his end and Chance blew out a breath.

"Will he fight?" Alexis asked.

"We might launch a couple of Nines like we did that first missile," she replied. "Let them coast for a bit, then send them through that. The Leviathan would have to turn on all their scanners to engage, so we'd see them as soon as they realized we'd taken another shot at them. At that point, I'd probably put four more Nines in the air with better targeting solutions and see if maybe we could hit that Leviathan hard enough to put them out of action for long enough to get away."

"Would he stay to kill them?" Alexis asked.

"He might," Chance said.

34

Padraig studied the plot Chance had delivered. Much smaller piece of the pie to work with. He sent it to Nyssa.

"Taggart, I want you to center your Survey equipment here and see if you can see anything at all," he ordered. "Leave everything else on general, passive scan, but you have the extra equipment today. Let's use it."

"Aye, sir," she replied.

Chance had included her notes about a salvo of Nines into the area, but Padraig had a better idea. Meaner, if nothing else.

She was right about having to turn on their targeting systems to engage nine fragments of a missile coming at them. That meant that he could better aim a Six or even a Three if he wanted.

That siren call was loud in the back of his head.

Coast a second missile for a time, since Maddox had already figured out an easy way to override the default programming on a missile. Get it turned and racing inwards on the target while *Marrakesh* was loaded up and ready to fire all six tubes in rapid sequence.

The problem was that both ships should have spent this entire time with the Ghostdrives reset and ready to jump up and away. The Leviathan could decide not to stay and play.

At that point, they would be running away from him, but if the other captain was smart, they'd plot an escape and evasion course that kept them between *Marrakesh* and any safe route back to Albany.

That was what he would have done if the situation were reversed.

Padraig had to assume that the other captain was at least competent, to have been put in command of a Leviathan.

And all the luck so far had been on Padraig's side of the equation. At some point, the other person would get lucky.

Still, he studied the new map. So much smaller, though that was only relative. And too much assumed that the gunboat had flown directly away from the Leviathan on launch, then maintained that heading.

If they hadn't, he was back to the larger sphere on the map, a massive pearl of uncertainty.

Still, he could smell the desperation in the air, like flop sweat.

"Nevin," he said abruptly, causing his Weapons Officer to look up sharply. "As soon as the Leviathan turns on their targeting systems, fire all six tubes on a reciprocal course. Program them to split early, sacrificing top speed for a wider impact zone, because we cannot stand and slug it out with them. Since we have a pretty good idea where they might be, that's an extra second we have to work with. Questions?"

"Negative, sir," Maddox replied.

Padraig dialed a number on his comm.

"Engineering. Ahearn."

"Ahearn, how quickly can you activate the Ghostdrives?" Padraig asked.

"Thirty seconds to transition, sir," Jareth Ahearn replied with a smile in his voice. "Been keeping them warm all this time. Later, we'll need to pull maintenance and swap out some parts, but I figured we were better off burning the quarterly budget today."

"Excellent news, Jareth," Padraig replied. "Stand by for a bit, but we might be approaching endgame on this one."

"Understood, Captain."

Padraig cut the line.

He felt it in his bones. That line in the sand marked *Diminishing Returns*, where it had gotten as good as it was going to, and every moment he stretched past this stacked the odds a little higher against him.

He hadn't run out of time, but the clock was ticking down.

One last time, Padraig pulled up Maddox's load-out on missiles, as well as the current aiming points of the turrets.

Did he dare initiate the final battle by turning on all his own targeting systems and firing?

He'd have surprise. And a better estimate of where to be facing in those critical moments.

Not yet though. Everyone was hyped by the missile that had blasted by at high speed.

He'd give them a few minutes to relax.

Not enough to unwind but looking forward to a break.

Yes. Looking away from their screens.

35

Kaitlin's butt was asleep. Well, partly asleep. These seats weren't designed for her butt. Nope, made for someone with a skinny ass that had no padding. Set wrong under her.

She got up and stretched, taking a moment to bend double and touch her toes as all the kinks in her back popped loose like corn kernels over heat.

The hatch to the A-module slid open, then closed.

"It's too early to do PT," Den called with a laugh as he approached.

Just because, Kaitlin held the stance a little longer, looking at the man upside down with an impertinent scowl.

"Do you good, Den," she replied after a beat, still upside down.

"I'd hurt myself trying," he nodded soberly.

Probably would. Man was all muscle, but solid and stolid. Blocky, rather than fluid.

Kaitlin unfolded and studied the Docker.

"Got any particular reason to be harshing my mellow, Den?" she asked with a grin.

Den turned deadly serious in the blink of an eye.

"Maybe something," he replied. "Maybe nothing."

Kaitlin felt her own systems dial up a notch.

"Talk to me," she ordered.

"I was down cycling through parts and stuff," he said. "One of the boxes hadn't been latched down fully when I stuck my head in, but I remember everything being to code earlier, because it would have stood out to me then."

"Somebody got into a box and didn't fully close it afterwards?" she asked, suddenly leaning forward on the balls of her feet.

"That's my read, but I've had my people shadowing all of Borsheva's people," Den nodded. "Not obviously, except that most of them are smart folks, so they might have figured something out. None of my people are friendly enough with them to spill the story, though. Nobody has broken loose from that."

Kaitlin paused to review things.

"What was in the box?" she asked.

"Electronics parts," Den nodded. "I didn't pull it out and make a big fuss about doing an inventory. Figured it was better to tell you immediately, so I left it exactly as it was and came up and over."

Kaitlin nodded. Anyone being sneaky getting into that equipment was up to no good. And that really only meant one thing at this point, at least in her mind.

"Where is it?" she asked.

"Deck Two, Room Three," he replied. "Want me to show you?"

"No," Kaitlin replied. "I want you to stay here like I've taken a potty break so you can keep watch. I'll go look at what you saw. Nothing unusual is happening, okay?"

Took him a second, then his face lit up.

"Gotcha, boss," he said.

Kaitlin watched him slide into the chair, wondering how long until it put his butt to sleep. She crossed over to the Gunnery module and looked around at the faces looking back.

Two crews. Well, halves of two crews, with her folks mixed in with Borsheva's. Half were up a deck in the turret itself, ready to fight if Padraig needed them. She'd put her foot down early and split the crews, explaining at the time that Borsheva's people needed to be ready to move at any moment, which meant that they couldn't all be asleep at the same time.

Thus, mixed and matched.

Nods greeted her. Folks here were reading, chatting, or studying for some upcoming qualification exam, so she waved and opened the hatch to drop down a deck.

Down.

Deck One was the docking mechanism itself, plus the generators that could drive the particle cannons and other equipment. Ammunition boxes were up on Six, with more stored on Three. Four was crew quarters, batteries, and capacitors.

She made it to Two without seeing anyone, but there weren't that many people around. A few would be napping on Four or over in the Survey module.

Nobody should have a reason to be down here.

She crossed the deck and located the storeroom Den had indicated. Racks stacked deck to ceiling, filled with smaller boxes, most of them transparent plastic so you could see the contents without having to open them.

Since she knew what to look for, Den's box immediately stood out, but Kaitlin doubted that any civilian would have noticed the difference. Their lives didn't depend on everything heavy being locked down, latched up, or held in a cargo net when the ship lost power and gravity.

It didn't happen all that often, but it did happen. Usually, in fact, when she ordered everything to be turned off so she could dock or remove a module, where the extra variable of locally generated gravity wasn't worth the effort.

But one was out of alignment. And looked like the latch hadn't been snapped all the way down, then the spring had flicked it open again, letting the box shift all of about half a centimeter. When the rest of the wall was almost as flat as a dance floor.

Kaitlin let the hatch close behind her and moved to the box. Latches undocked and it came out. She pulled the lid and looked inside.

None of it was navy gear, so she had to pull unlabeled cardboard boxes out. Topmost one was empty by weight in her hand.

Had somebody pulled the contents, stuffed them in a pocket, then put the box back?

Kaitlin studied the side of the box, but the label was a hash-code. She'd need to poll the inventory database to know what it had held.

She closed the lid with the empty in her other hand, locked everything, then latched it down. For now, Kaitlin left the larger box on the deck at her feet and pulled out her cargo reader. On came the light and she scanned the hashcode.

All that gave her was a catalog number, so she had to shift around and start looking up parts in the system, grumbling under her breath as she did. Damned civilians didn't even use the same database technology, so she had to copy the part numbers, then paste them into a different screen.

And copied it wrong, since she was pretty sure that the box

hadn't held parts for a rotary thruster cooling system. Especially not one that outmassed her.

More grumbles.

There.

Okay.

She got it right this time, having left off a decimal at the end the first time. Short-range scanner module replacement parts. Engineering stuff. Civilian, but close enough to what the navy used.

Uh huh. Hmmmm.

Oh, shit.

The device wasn't self-contained, but did include a short-range radio transmitter, designed to immediately off-load data to a larger system that could make sense of them.

Ten thousand data points weren't worth shit until you could plot them on a curve and see trends, after all.

The radio part was what concerned her. She'd spoken with Chance in coded terms. She and Nyssa Taggart had hopefully cooked up a scheme, but Kaitlin hadn't been in a position to ask for details.

It was enough in her mind to know that smart people had taken the threat seriously enough to do something about it.

Kaitlin nodded. She could look up the frequencies that the device was intended to broadcast on and let Chance know. Hopefully, they could block those without making a stink.

She'd really like to not get her ass shot off today. Especially since it was finally awake again.

Kaitlin was about to put everything back how she'd found it—except put in correctly this time—when the hatch opened.

She looked up, expecting Den or one of his people making a periodic sweep for security sake.

Ryan Donal stood there instead. Frozen in shock to see her

standing there, holding the small box with the big one at her feet.

Then the panic hit and he turned and started running without saying a word.

Kaitlin dropped everything and took off after the man.

All of Borsheva's people were being quietly shadowed by hers.

Except one.

Probably because, like her, he was kind of a free agent.

How much so remained to be seen.

The hatch to the stairs opened, and she heard steps thundering away from her as Dr. Donal seemed to be getting away.

Kaitlin started after him.

Not on my watch, bucko.

36

Kaitlin wasn't built for speed. Short, broad, tough, strong.

And stubborn as hell.

But not built for running.

Still, she wasn't about to give this yahoo any advantage, especially as he had nowhere to run once he stopped and thought about it. The outer hatches were locked tight and had armed goons making sure nobody opened them.

Internally, most things were locked down as well.

But the man had seen what she was doing and bolted. Hadn't even tried to play it off with some bullshit song and dance routine.

Just run.

In her mind, Kaitlin assumed that he'd built the device, and had come back to get a second piece, one to maybe extend the range or something, uncertain how that mass of charged blue fog around them might mess up any signal he wanted to send.

She couldn't think of any other reason to bolt, save to get back to the device he'd built and trigger it now, before someone tackled him.

Worse, she hadn't stopped to hit the intercom so someone might intercept the man above.

She'd run blindly after him.

Kaitlin didn't outmass the man, though it might be close. She was damned certain that she could outlift him.

If she could catch him.

She growled at the universe and pushed herself as she heard him go.

Somewhere above, a hatch slid open, and Donal's footsteps got quieter as he left the stairwell. The hatch closed again, but she had placed him in her mind.

All those years of three-dimensional problem solving for a living.

He'd exited on Five. Had she been closer, she might have gotten one of her sailors to intercept the man.

Had she been thinking, they might have been poised at the hatch, waiting like a pack of mangy coyotes.

Okay, maybe *mangy* was a bit rude, even for sailors.

Still…

She hit Five and the hatch slid open for her. Kaitlin went through the opening like a whirlwind, idly noting the folks sitting around and watching her dumbfounded.

A few of her people caught on and started to rise, but she was already across the room, where the crossover hatch was sliding shut.

Good. She'd been afraid the man would get to Deck Six and maybe figure out a way to fire one of those guns. Shouldn't be possible, at least not with navy gear, but this was an experimental installation, so she couldn't say for certain.

Especially not if someone was desperate enough.

Given how fast Donal was running, he was.

The airlock hatches didn't need to cycle. She hit the near

one just starting to slide shut as the far one was already open. Ryan Donal looked back over his shoulder, and she saw that first hint of fear in his eyes, still too far away to stop the man.

He kept running, wordless.

She chased.

Kaitlin got to the other hatch and saw Donal moving laterally towards the stairs down. He must have hidden whatever it was in his bunk. Good place for it, as he had a cabin to himself. Not much larger than a coffin, exactly like hers when she wasn't over in the main hull, but private.

Exactly what you needed to commit treason?

He was going to get there. She wasn't built for speed.

Kaitlin Lynch was, however, built for sneaky.

"Den, stop him!" she yelled as soon as she saw the scene.

She would never forget the response as long as she lived.

Den Gilroy, Docker and senior-most enlisted crew in the cargo department. Good *feng shui* on his visible tattoos. Adjustment wrench down by his side as he sat. Goofball and three-quarters most of the time, except when it became necessary to measure the mobile geometry of a load of several thousand tons in millimeters.

Den looked at her. Looked at Donal. Turned deadly serious.

He rotated in his seat to shift his left shoulder back ninety degrees, bringing the wrench up and over, then throwing it like an ax.

She blinked in surprise and almost tripped herself, but managed to hold on as the silver blur spiraled across the room and took Donal out at the knee, tangling both of his feet.

Man face-planted into a bulkhead when he missed the opening hatch to the stairwell. Sounded like someone had hit a bell with a cantaloupe from the dull, ringing echo.

She hoped that he hadn't just broken his fool neck, but she would deal with that later.

"Den, get over here," Kaitlin ordered as she slid the last meter on her knees.

Donal was out cold but breathing. Gonna have one hell of a lump on the top of his forehead, but he'd probably impacted at the safest spot to not kill himself, all things considered. Hard bones.

Den was there a moment later.

"Tape!" she said.

A roll of the heavy stuff appeared in her hand.

The tools of an engineer. Lubricant to make things go. Tape to make them stop.

She flipped Donal back onto his face for now, turning his head so he could breathe, and tacked both wrists together with several loops to hold them. They might need to get out some alcohol later to dissolve the adhesive, but that would be somebody else's problem.

"Watch him," Kaitlin ordered. "Medical as well as security."

"Got it," Den replied, one hand landing on Donal's back in a most proprietary manner.

After all, broken legs hadn't counted. That's what she'd told him at the start.

Kaitlin got up and staggered to the console, only now aware of how much her ankles hurt from all the running. Probably needed to spend more time each day racing madly up and down stairs.

"Secondary Bridge. Magorian."

"Bex, tell Chance I need two security teams aboard the Survey module immediately," Kaitlin said. "I've just taken Dr. Donal into custody, and he was up to something."

"Kaitlin, Chance here," the First Officer was suddenly on the line. "What's your situation?"

"Under control," Kaitlin replied. "But I think I need to take the rest of Borsheva's people into custody until we can sort everything out. Don't know if Donal was acting alone, but he sure is acting guilty as hell."

"Understood," Chance said. "I'll scramble folks for you and let Padraig know. Does he need to be there?"

"Not immediately," Kaitlin said. "There's still a bigger fish out there to fry."

"In motion," Chance said.

Kaitlin settled herself in the chair and let the adrenaline wear off some.

No chance in hell her butt was going to sleep now.

37

Chance played the message back for Padraig. Whatever Kaitlin had seen must have been damning, but she was also right that the Captain still had a Leviathan to deal with.

"Thoughts?" Chance asked when the playback was done.

"You and Borsheva go down with those teams," he replied. "They stay. Both of you return to Secondary when you're certain that things are under control. I'd rather apologize to all her people later, but I still want all of them in a couple of cabins on the ship and locked in. Kaitlin will have final say on when they get out. If they get out."

Chance gulped at the pure rage she heard in Padraig's voice but didn't say anything. Instead, she nodded to Alexis and keyed a circuit on her board.

"Security. Farrell."

"Cameron, I need you to scramble two security teams and meet me outside the hatch to the Survey module immediately," Chance said. "Stun weapons only at present."

"Understood, sir," the woman replied. "Got one team on

hot standby. Will need two minutes to get the other one in place."

"See you there," Chance said as she cut the line.

Then she drew a heavy breath and keyed a code into the drawer under her console, pausing to pull out an Adjustable Disruptor. Drawing the weapon from the holster, she dialed it all the way out to the broadest aperture, just to be sure.

Handheld miniature particle cannon, it could be set as tight as a welding laser, or broad to hit like a fist. Kaitlin sounded like she was safe, so Chance wasn't going to go in there like a samurai, set to open fire on anything that moved.

She was prepared anyway.

Chance rose and attached the holster to the equipment belt on the outside of her emergency suit, then locked eyes with Alexis.

"I still can't imagine Ryan doing something," Alexis whispered.

Chance shrugged. They'd bonded over the last day, but she'd only met the other man in passing and he hadn't been all that talkative.

They went down and forward.

Cameron Farrell had her team in place when they arrived, eight armed sailors, one of whom hadn't even taken off his apron from where he'd been prepping food in the wardroom.

Marrakesh had a full security force, but the ship was too small to let them be dedicated to training for combat, so they all had secondary jobs in the wardroom, engineering, or damage control.

Lead Farrell was the only one on permanent duty.

All were armed with disruptors like hers, in hand with the barrels pointed at the deck.

"Stun only?" Chance asked as she came up.

With these nine, plus the four that had already been on guard, the corridor was a little full.

"Everyone but me, sir," Cameron replied.

Chance started to say something, then caught herself. Yes, somebody probably did need to be ready to kill. Chance was just glad it didn't have to be her today.

She nodded instead.

"Open it up," she ordered. "Then lock it down to me or the Lead only. If you have a question, call Captain Boru."

The sailor nodded with a grim face and keyed the lock.

The hatch opened and Chance went in at the head of a small army.

38

Kaitlin had waited until Den led the mob of sailors up to Four, where she'd stashed the taped-up Donal in her own cabin to keep him out of trouble.

"Two and Three are clear, boss," Den said as he came out of the stairwell.

Kaitlin nodded and locked eyes with Lead Farrell. Kaitlin and Den were both short and compact. Broad in the body with muscles. Cameron Farrell might be mistaken for a guy in a dark room, standing one hundred and eighty-eight centimeters tall and massing more than ninety kilos.

Sometimes you find the job. Sometimes the job finds you.

"I need every cabin on this deck cleared of civilian personnel," Kaitlin ordered the woman. "Two of you back into the stairwell and nobody gets past you."

Bodies exploded into motion, leaving Kaitlin to stand around with Chance and Alexis.

A handful of civilians got roused from their sleep, dragged out in socks. One had been sleeping nude, but one of the troopers handed him pants for now. No shirt, because she hadn't said anything.

Might not.

She didn't know if Donal had friends, and her hatch was closed for now.

"What's going on?" one of the women asked, eyes still bleary from stress and lack of sleep.

"Trouble," Kaitlin growled. "Stay shut up until it gets sorted out."

That got attention, but seriously, the group of armed sailors should have done that.

"Den, you take Cameron and a team to clear Five, then hold at the airlock," Kaitlin ordered. "We'll follow with this mob."

Everyone sorted themselves out, and Kaitlin followed in about the middle of the group. Cameron was armed. Den had his wrench. Kaitlin wasn't worried.

Five was clear and everything locked down.

"One sailor remains here," Kaitlin ordered. "Nobody passes except me or the First Officer."

Alexis started to say something, then shut her mouth when Kaitlin turned her scowl on the woman.

Silence. Even the civilians were catching on that shit had just gotten real.

"Stun weapons," Kaitlin reminded everyone. "Last time I looked, there were more than a dozen folks lounging on the other side of this hatch. Half are sailors, but do not hesitate to fire if you have to stop a runner."

Kaitlin noted the way Cameron twisted her barrel. Woman had been on kill mode up until now and didn't want to be relegated to the back.

"Den, you stand aside," Cameron said. "I'm leading."

Den started to grumble but caught Kaitlin's eye and subsided.

The group went through the paired hatches less like a plague of locusts but more than a promenade.

Folks had jumped up, but in confusion, not stupidity. That was good. Nobody got shot as a result.

"*Marrakesh* crew to one side," Kaitlin ordered loudly. "Civilians, you are being taken into protective custody and removed from the module until such time as we can clarify a few things."

What, she left out. If they didn't know, they weren't spies. And she still had Ryan Donal to deal with once she got everyone else sorted out.

"Turret's a bit crowded, boss," Den reminded her.

Kaitlin considered it. Then she turned to Chance, trailing along quietly up until now, mostly babysitting Alexis.

"You're in charge here," Kaitlin said. "I'll be right back. Den, with me."

She didn't bother with a pistol. Den had his wrench, and there were half a dozen sailors up there that would join a brawl at the drop of a hat.

She went up a deck, focused on controlling her breathing. Ankles hurt. Butt was wide awake now. Obviously, she had been slacking on the PT before this and would need to catch up. Probably have to make life hell for her sailors for a while, exercising more and harder.

They'd all volunteered for this job.

The turret was designed for three barrels and firing mechanisms, but only had the outer two, with controls and sensor equipment in the middle. Men and women stood around, perking up as she entered the space.

"Surprise party down on Five," Kaitlin announced. "Civilians get first crack at the cake. Sailors will go down after you folks have your fill. Den, you're in charge up here."

She did appreciate the good-natured teasing from the civilians. Meant that they thought she was on the level. And the truth would flip things nicely.

Kaitlin led the half dozen civilians down to Five, where Cameron and her people had guns pointed at them when they emerged.

"What the hell?" one of them managed before Cameron grabbed the smaller guy and dragged him to one side bodily.

Bigger. Stronger. Tougher. Meaner.

"Ladies and gentlemen, you are being taken into protective custody," Kaitlin announced. "The First Officer will see you to new quarters in the main part of the ship. Questions will not be answered, so don't try my patience by asking. Chance? Cameron?"

"This way," Lead Farrell growled. Twenty civilians. Nine troopers. Not even remotely fair if some fool started something, because the cook looked like he was feeling cannibalistic right at the moment.

Kaitlin didn't ask.

Instead, she waited until they got the civilians cleared. There were a few of her people sleeping below that would be picked up, then the two modules would be limited to sailors Kaitlin trusted.

She walked to the intercom and dialed. Easier if everyone heard it at once.

"Bridge. Boru."

"Situation under control here, Padraig," she said. "Chance and Cameron have them and will haul Donal down so you can throw him in the brig. I'll go back and toss his quarters with

Den in a bit, and I've got sufficient crew to man the guns for now, but sleeping schedules will put a cramp on things."

"Understood, Kaitlin," Padraig replied. "I think that this will be resolved, one way or the other, in a few hours at the outside, so let your folks know I need effort that long, then we're in Ghost-space and running like hell."

"Thanks, Padraig," Kaitlin said.

She cut the line and turned to the sailors around her.

"You heard it," she said. "Donal looks like he was a spy. I'm going to go see. We're all pulling doubles at this point, so make sure you potty now, then head aloft and give them a break as well."

Bodies exploded into action.

Kaitlin headed over to the survey module to see if she could find the gadget that had started it all.

39

———————

Chance supervised moving the civilians into a set of empty cabins that were overflow for the most part. Cruiser hulls were built to a particular size to make them easier to maintain and repair, but a Tactical Transport like *Marrakesh* had only about half of the crew.

And folks hadn't been allowed to spread out so that everyone got their own. Enlisted still hotbunked double until they reached E6 Lead. There was space, because Padraig hadn't let folks start using the empties as storage, either.

"Alexis, why?" the last of the folks asked as they all got herded into too small a space for the eight of them.

"I can't tell you," Alexis said.

Chance heard the pain in the woman's voice but didn't know if it was the potential betrayal of Ryan Donal, or the empathy of fear from her people being potentially subject to Navy justice.

Captain Padraig Boru was like a god while he commanded a starship in service. They'd all signed the necessary forms to bring them under military control for the time being.

Now, they might find out what that actually meant.

Cameron locked the hatch, then detailed one of her teams to watch it, having pulled folks from guarding the modules for now.

"Donal next?" the Lead asked.

"Yes," Chance replied. "He's going directly to the brig."

Back aft. In. Up. Kaitlin was watching the man. He was awake, but still looked a little glassy eyed from the concussion.

"Do we need medical first?" Chance asked.

She technically out-ranked Kaitlin, but this was Kaitlin's gig.

"Probably wouldn't hurt," Kaitlin replied, explaining what Den Gilroy had done to stop Donal's flight.

Cameron picked him up off the bunk. Kaitlin produced a small shell with electronics and wires.

"I still have the battery, so it can't send a signal, but this is what I found in his cabin," Kaitlin said. "Nyssa Taggart or one of her people can tell you if it would work."

Chance studied it for a long moment, turning the thing over in her hands.

"It should, but I can see where he was trying to add an amplifier to boost the signal," Chance said.

Kaitlin and Alexis both stared at her, surprised.

"Desk job for several years," she reminded them. "And I wasn't sure at the time that command slots would open up again. This was before the latest war, so I took some electronics classes in case I needed to transfer to Survey Command."

Nods.

Wronlori might have finally decided to grow up. At least that had been the hope when the *Holy Imperium of Copez* got a new Archbishop and broke with *Wronlori* six years ago, after the end of the *War of the Third Alliance* two years before that.

It hadn't worked out that way, but she was aboard *Marrakesh.* And learning a lot more about starship command from Padraig Boru than she'd ever expected.

Chance turned to Cameron's prisoner.

"Feel like talking?" she asked, mostly to see if he would.

Donal glowered at her rather impressively for a man whose eyes were a little crossed still.

"Your prisoner," Chance told Cameron. "Someone with him at all times until Doc clears him. After medical, swap the tape for manacles, but keep his hands behind him after you get him out of those clothes."

She turned to Kaitlin as Chance led the man away.

"Have you tossed the place fully?" she asked.

"I have not," Kaitlin replied with a head shake. "Wanted folks here that might recognize things I'd miss. Like Alexis."

"I'm not a suspect?" Alexis asked.

"If you're a spy, too, then we have far bigger problems," Chance replied. "Folks back home will probably end up going over your ass with a microscope, but that will be incidental to taking Ryan Donal's entire life apart to figure out how he was able to get into this situation without someone catching him before this."

"Oh."

"So, let's dig," Chance said to Kaitlin, grabbing the bunk and pulling sheets.

Kaitlin went for the footlocker and pulled everything out, dumping it on the stripped bed as Alexis stayed out of the way, crammed into the corner.

Small cabin. Three people standing up was too many.

"What's this?" Chance said as a book bounced off the mattress and a piece of folded paper slipped out.

She studied it but didn't recognize the language. Everybody

used the same written language, made up of letters to form words, but the dialects and pronunciations varied widely.

Still wasn't anything she knew.

"Kaitlin? Alexis?"

Both women looked over her shoulder as Chance held it out.

"Looks like trouble," Alexis said. "Almost like some sort of code that might be transmitted?"

Chance squinted.

"Maybe?" she offered.

Then she flipped the book itself over. A trashy medical thriller, from the art and the blurb. Not anything she knew, but Chance had been busy with books for Xandra and Daneel for the last several years as they learned to read.

She put it to one side, along with the paper.

Nothing else seemed interesting, but Chance also knew that none of them were JAG investigators. She picked up the book, the paper, and the transmitter.

"Lock the room up tight, Kaitlin," she said. "This can wait until we get home for the Judge Advocate General professionals to search. I think we've got the important parts for now. And the transmitter itself is probable cause to hold Donal in the brig."

"What will happen to him?" Alexis asked nervously.

"Depends," Chance replied. "If he's a *Wronlori* spy, the law might have him executed. More likely he'd be imprisoned for a long time. Maybe traded. Not anything I know. Right now, he is no longer a threat to *Marrakesh* and the crew, and that's all I really care about."

"What about me?" Alexis asked.

Chance turned to Kaitlin. Her bailiwick.

"We could use your expertise if we have to fight," Kaitlin

offered. "It will only be my people, and while they are trained, they aren't going to be as good as yours if something goes wrong."

"Oh," Alexis nodded. "I can do that."

Chance nodded as well.

"You folks are on your own," she told them. "I'll go forward and brief Padraig, then see where we are with that Leviathan."

Chance slipped out of the room and headed down while they went up.

This much they had dealt with.

And it was still only a sideshow.

40

Padraig listened to Chance's story as they sat in his office with the door closed.

"And at that point, we're better off than we had been, but we'll need JAG to handle things, so I had Kaitlin lock it up."

"Exactly right," he agreed.

"What are you planning from here?" Chance asked.

He grimaced, but she needed to know, in case something happened. They hadn't known each other before she'd been assigned as his First Officer and were still sorting things out.

Plus, she'd been flying a desk for nearly seven years, and was still getting her sea legs under her again.

"I could run," he told her. "Just to Ghost-space and hope that the drives hold us all the way back to Albany."

"They've launched their wolfpack," Chance pointed out. "Couldn't we escape?"

"We could," he acknowledged. "They either remain behind to retrieve them, or immediately chase after us, hopefully all the way back to base. Without those gunboats, I don't think they can threaten us once we get close enough to the station."

"But?" she asked, eyes locked.

"I'm maybe a wee bit too grumpy about having been chased out here in the first place," he grinned. "I'd like to hurt them if I can. Up until now, we've tried a number of things, both to hide and to spook them. We do have a rough sphere where we think the Leviathan ought to be, but it's still huge."

"Too rough to launch a wave into it and hope?" Chance asked him.

"Too big," he nodded. "Chances of a hit are low."

"Any way we can even them up a little?" she pressed.

"Now that you've solved a potential spy issue, I have more space to breathe," he nodded. "Thank you, because I think I get to turn Maddox Nevin loose and see what he can do."

"What should I be doing?" Chance nodded back.

"What you have been doing," he smiled. "Backing me up and out-thinking bad guys. From here, it will turn into a very short pitched battle. Then we're finally running for home."

She rose.

"I'll swing by and let Ahearn know," she said. "He'll want some warning in case he has to pull something apart to fix it."

"You do that," Padraig said, also rising.

"Can we pull it off?" she asked as they stood facing each other.

"I intend to try."

41

Padraig settled in his big, comfortable chair and hooked the strap to hold him in.

First, he turned to Nyssa Taggart.

"Any recent indications of enemy warships?" he asked. "Even ghosts?"

"Nothing that rises to the level of even uncertainty, sir," Nyssa replied crisply. "We have the original coordinates from the First Officer, but that's it."

Padraig nodded.

He'd hoped, but both sides were handling this like professionals. He'd gotten the one bit of luck. Well, far more than one, with the gunboat unmasking itself and a possible spy caught, but the one was what he was counting on.

Padraig turned to Maddox Nevin next.

"Weapons, I want you to reprogram one of the Nines in the tubes," he ordered. "Give it a three-minute delay from the catapult, then reorient and aim it at the expected current coordinates of the gunboat we scanned earlier. Go for a kill there."

"Aye, sir," Maddox replied. "Nine. Three minutes. Target designated *beta*."

"Then have Tindal reload with a Six," Padraig continued, turning his attention to Zarah Halloran. "Helm, once we launch that Nine, you will rotate the ship on gyroscopes and maneuvering thrusters to bring us stern-on with the calculated coordinates of the Leviathan. I want a Parthian shot over our shoulder, where the bow turret can come to bear, so down and about one hundred and ten degrees from current."

"Parthian shot, aye, sir," Zarah nodded. "The A-turret can arc one-twenty-five at current standing. Is one-fifteen acceptable?"

"It is," Padraig nodded. "Nevin, when your Nine fires, you will be prepared to empty all six tubes, centering them across the Leviathan's calculated location. All three heavy particle cannon turrets will be centered for fire as soon as they have a target, with all four defensive turrets set to engage the other gunboats as they appear, or missiles in flight. Same with the railgun pulsars. Questions?"

"Ready to engage as soon as we have a vector, Captain," Maddox smiled.

Padraig nodded.

Good crew, and they were coming together better and faster than he'd hoped.

Trial by fire would do that.

Trial by Leviathan would do it even better. Assuming they survived.

He keyed the ship-wide intercom.

"All hands, this is your Captain," he spoke smoothly. "In ten minutes, we will launch an attack against our foes, so I need everyone steady and prepared to give me everything they have. It won't take long, then we'll be running like hell for safety, since a Tactical Transport like *Marrakesh* should never engage a *Wronlori* Leviathan in the first place. But I wanted all of you to know that we intend to take a bite out of them before we go. Captain out."

He cut the line and noted all the smiles around him.

Two incredible days of stress and craziness, and it was coming down to this.

He couldn't wait.

42

BRIDGE, SUNDERING WRATH

Divna had taken another break, but they had gotten shorter in duration. Captain Boru had to be getting desperate by now.

The display was optical on the main screen, while the officers around her studied scans or other things. Divna liked the blue fog. If not for the situation around them, she would have found it soothing.

Instead, the hue had begun to wear on her.

Maric must have sensed something because he turned his attention to her.

"Marshal?" he asked in a private voice.

"There is a timer running in the back of my head, Captain," she replied, equally quiet. "It tells me that we are coming down to the end of this spectacle."

"Do we turn on all the sensors and dare *Marrakesh* to fight us?" he asked.

Divna held her reply. There would be a stretch of time where they were blind, while *Marrakesh* would be able to see them, as the signal propagated. In that time, Boru could launch missiles before *Sundering Wrath* could reply.

Worse, depending on relative positions and alignments, they might be able to open fire in those first, critical seconds.

Marrakesh was testing experimental, long-range, heavy particle cannons, after all.

How long-range?

"It may come to that," she nodded. "Not yet, but I can't help but sense that it will be soon."

Maric nodded and subsided.

Peace filled the bridge, with that mesmerizing blue haze just out the window.

"Sensors," a female voice rang out. "I have contact!"

As before, Divna felt the surge of adrenaline grip her like a lover.

Finally!

43

Padraig watched the countdown timer on his board.

He made eye contact with Maddox, and they shared a silent nod.

Shortly.

Padraig turned to Nyssa.

"As soon as that missile lights, they will detect it," he reminded her. "I want you to make sure every scanner you have is watching in that moment when they are confused, so you can give Maddox's people hard vectors of engagement. We're going to give them everything we've got, as fast as we can."

"Standing by, sir," Nyssa nodded coolly.

"Helm, status?" he asked next.

"Ready to run, sir," Zarah replied. "Ahearn is prepared to flit us out as soon as you give the order."

"Thirty seconds, Captain," Maddox said.

Padraig drew a breath and considered the insanity of what he was about to do.

At the same time, nobody would expect it, and he figured

he had an even chance to catch the Leviathan facing the wrong direction, or at least unable to reply immediately.

With any luck, they'd be too far away to fire back, and facing wrong with their lower deck turned to him like a turtle's belly. Twenty extra seconds to roll to bring their own guns to bear.

Anything.

"Ten seconds to missile one," Maddox reminded everyone.

Padraig blew out that breath and settled himself deeper into his chair.

He could still run. Still get away if things went wrong.

But he wanted to bite that bastard at least once before he left.

Remind them that *A'Zedi* hadn't started any of the last several wars. They had merely pushed *Wronlori* bullies back or at least held the line.

"Missile ignition confirmed," Nyssa called to the room. "Sensors coming live now."

"All batteries, engage anything as you bear," Padraig called over the intercom.

If that Leviathan was close enough for the defensive turrets to hit them, he wanted them pouring fire in now. Missile defense could come after that.

"Contact!" Nyssa called. "Four enemy warships. Leviathan and three gunboats confirmed."

Padraig looked at his echo of her board.

Not the worst outcome. Not the best. High and a little left of the space Chance and Dr. Borsheva had predicted, but that had been hours ago, so they might have drifted. Plus, his people had been guessing, based solely on the placement of the one gunboat they'd seen for two seconds.

Pretty damned good, otherwise.

That one gunboat was just about dead center on the track of the Nine as the missile accelerated downrange. They'd have to be lucky to not take at least one fragment when it separated. Might take two if Maddox caught it just right on corners.

Both sides of the ship rattled as the first pair of tubes catapulted their birds into space. No lag here. Four seconds, rotation, ignition.

Starship combat, pure and simple.

"Weapons module, I have lock," Den Gilroy's voice came over the line from Maddox's station. "Engaging now."

"Forward turret, engaging."

"Aft guns locked and firing."

"Second salvo away. First flight ignited and tracking true."

"Battery Three, I have a gunboat at outer range. Engaging until they launch a missile back at us. Railgun teams, track this vector."

"Battery Four, standing by to receive enemy fire."

"Battery One, gunboat *gamma* is spinning to bring their turret to bear defensively. Engaging."

"Third flight away. First two tracking."

"Separation on that surprise Nine. Tracking against gunboat *beta*. We appear to have surprise."

Padraig's bridge was forward, but deep inside the ship, to the point that none of the weapons made any noise he could detect. Instead, he had learned to listen to the small earthquakes that rattled the hull as big and little turrets rotated. The contained explosion as particle cannons ignited their shells and focused the resulting beam downrange. The hard thump of catapults tossing heavy missiles clear of the hull.

Marrakesh wiggled like a hound that had just climbed out of the bath, shaking itself to get all the water off.

Padraig sat as still as he could and tried to will calmness to his officers and crew. They needed to know that all of this was going exactly according to plan.

Close enough. That Leviathan had been facing wrong. Not perfectly flat for them to shoot at, but not edge on, either. Surprised, though, because it took them nearly eight seconds to activate their own targeting sensors.

That first gunboat had just enough time to light everything when a shard of a Nine passed through the bow like an arrow spiking a catfish to the board for cleaning.

Except catfish never exploded when you did that.

"Weapons, status on your missiles?" Padraig asked, focusing on sounding calm and collected as he spoke.

"Tracking true, sir," Maddox replied, voice bouncing all over the place in his excitement.

Padraig nodded coolly. Maddox's first ever engagement in charge of the big guns and missiles. Padraig remembered his first on *Nemesis*.

"Helm, ahead full on your rotary thrusters," Padraig ordered. "Get me some space, then stand by to transition, but hold for my order. We still have an edge, and I plan to exploit it."

"Ahead full and holding for Ghostdrives," Zarah called back firmly, hands dancing across her controls.

Padraig smiled when Den Gilroy got a hit with the weapon's module. Heavy and hard, catching the Leviathan a slash across the bow armor and possibly nailing one of their forward main turrets, from the sudden jet of plasma and atmosphere that erupted.

Secondary explosion from an ammunition hit? They weren't impossible, but it required a great deal of luck.

Someone aft had laid that third shot almost exactly right.

The Leviathan seemed to suffer an earthquake as Padraig watched.

Marrakesh shuddered on a different pitch.

"Incoming fire from gunboat *delta*," Maddox spoke aloud, but sounded professional again. "Rear armor is absorbing it at present."

"Has the Leviathan locked on with their main guns?" Padraig asked Nyssa.

"Affirmative," she replied. "I have a solid lock inbound, ranging us now."

Padraig nodded. He'd gotten a couple of thumping hits home to open the conversation. Hurt them, but he wouldn't know how well until later, when Nyssa could review her logs.

"All guns, continue to engage," Padraig ordered, a new timer counting down in his own head until he had no choice but to run.

Marrakesh couldn't defeat a Leviathan, even with surprise and luck.

But he'd take what he could get. That captain over there would remember him for this.

Would remember the name *Marrakesh*.

"Leviathan is ranging fire," Nyssa called. "First salvo was high."

"They fired too soon," Padraig replied to her. "The ship over there is rotating to bring their edge on to us. Smaller target for our guns. Someone lost track of that in maneuvering."

She blinked, then nodded.

This was why he'd ordered Zarah to push them away, but not to start the sorts of wild evasive maneuvering that the Leviathan was undergoing.

"Captain, we have reloaded the first set of missile tubes," Maddox called. "Do we continue launching?"

Padraig studied the plot. The Leviathan was rotating and getting ready to bring their four triple Heavy turrets to bear, against his pitiful three twins that *Marrakesh* could answer with. Overload, when they got that broadside locked in and started pounding his boat to scrap.

At the same time, they had only now started to engage incoming missiles and fragments with their own defensive batteries and railgun pulsars.

Could he overload them?

"Taggart, what's their A-turret doing?" he asked her.

A-turret. B-turret. Z-turret and Y-turret counting inwards from the stern. Some real monsters added a C- and X-turret on top of that.

Marrakesh had one forward and one aft, with four smaller, defensive batteries on the corners.

Nyssa leaned forward on her board, and Padraig held his breath.

"A-turret is not rotating, Captain," she said. "B-turret is, but not as quickly as the rear ones."

Shit, Den must have cut power or something with his hit, and the *Wronlori* damage control team hadn't gotten a new line spliced in quickly. Which might take minutes.

Had that Leviathan just lost half of its firepower?

First rule of combat: always go for the throat.

"Nevin, continue launching," Padraig ordered. "Reload with Threes and keep that Leviathan too busy defending itself. All batteries not engaging gunboats directly prepare to receive enemy missiles."

Two gunboats remained, both out of position and slewing around. One had died in a flash of pretty orange plasma. The fourth remained docked to the Leviathan, so they must have hit it harder than they'd thought yesterday.

Yesterday? Felt like a week ago.

"Missile separation confirmed," Maddox replied. "First flight tracking true. Enemy defensive fire engaging our missiles."

Padraig would have liked one or a pair of missile modules aft. He only had six tubes to that Leviathan's eight. Eighteen would have been a nice surprise.

"Enemy missiles launched and tracking," Nyssa's voice overrode.

"Batteries engaging now at the outer envelope."

Padraig slammed his mouth shut and let his people work.

"Oh, shit, we've got a probable!" Maddox called, voice rising with excitement.

Padraig switched views to what his Weapons Officer was seeing.

The Sixes had caught them off guard. Too many fragments, all closing at high speed and accurate enough to be a threat with neither ship moving much relative to each other.

Those ten seconds might have meant the difference.

Defensive batteries and railgun pulsars were firing over there for all they were worth, but there were too many things coming in.

A fragment caught the Leviathan a glancing blow. Still, several tons of high speed, irresistible force meeting unmovable object.

Except that it could move. Armor was only so good. Physics got involved as mass and velocity got converted to plasma energy and rotational torque.

The starboard stern corner of the Leviathan vanished in a flash of light that needed nearly a second to cool down from blue hot invisibility to a bright white explosion.

Pretty, against the blue skies that had been his life for what felt like forever.

Then the Leviathan vanished.

44

BRIDGE, SUNDERING WRATH

Divna felt an earthquake rattle through the entire hull. It was like standing inside a giant bell that had just been struck with a log at one of the ancient temples back home. The impact threw her to the ground in spite of a hand locked on to the edge of the console in front of her.

Around her, the lights went out for a moment, then came back on at half strength. Emergency backups with the mains down.

She smelled smoke. Usually the second worst thing that could happen on any starship, behind only wind from a hull breach.

"Status!" Divna heard Maric call over the babble of voices around her.

"Missile hit, sir," someone called. "There are more inbound."

"Run!" Divna called, getting as far as shaky knees.

Maric looked at her with blind, confused eyes.

"Go to Ghostdrive now!" Divna yelled as loudly as she could. "Flit while we can still escape with our lives."

Someone heard her, because the ship blipped out a moment later, nearly tossing her back on her ass as she was trying to stand up.

Maric caught her arm and held her as she steadied.

"I need a medical team to the bridge!" he yelled, still staring at her.

Divna felt something warm on her forehead. A hand came up and touched it.

Red. Blood. Hers.

"The Marshal has been injured," Maric called loudly to the room.

A crew member appeared from somewhere with a medkit in hand. They put her right back down on the deck, cold on her bottom as all her senses seemed at once to be dulled by a layer of cotton batting and hyperalertness.

A towel blinded her for a moment. Or maybe it was her blood. She remembered from somewhere that head wounds tended to bleed worse than anywhere else. Veins on the surface, with solid bone beneath, so it couldn't bleed internally.

The woman held up fingers.

Divna found it difficult to track them as they moved around.

"I have a probable concussion here," Divna heard her say, as if from another room. "Marshal, stay with me. You've been injured, but we'll take care of you."

"The ship," she said.

Tried to say. It came out as more of a croak than anything. Still, Captain Maric squatted down next to her.

"Marshal?"

"The ship," Divna tried again, one hand flailing outward to point. Indicate. Something.

"We have transitioned to Ghostdrives, Marshal," he said.

"At present, we are withdrawing. The gunboats will follow as soon as they realize, then we will rendezvous at the designated location."

She nodded.

Luck. That's what it was. *Sundering Wrath* had gotten the short end of it today, but they had escaped, however bad the damage must be forward.

"How is she?" a new male crew member asked, brushing Maric aside to stare at her owlishly.

Divna felt owlish. Her head rotated fine, but her eyes didn't want to. Her ears rang terribly, overwhelming other sound and making it almost impossible to follow conversations.

"Serious concussion," the first woman said. "Laceration on the skull but I don't think the bone cracked."

"Too hard-headed," Divna laughed at the thought. That was what they'd always said about her.

Too damned stubborn.

The man touched the side of her neck with something.

Coolness spread out and she felt her muscles relaxing from the rigidity she hadn't even realized was there.

A nap sounded good.

They helped her lay flat, and darkness claimed her.

45

Padraig nodded as the Leviathan vanished. That hit might have broken a ship like *Marrakesh* into two pieces. Leviathans were beasts.

"Weapons, track the gunboats and continue engaging," he ordered, just in case someone wondered. "Do we have inbound missiles?"

"Two," Nyssa called.

Padraig saw them as vectors on his echo of her board.

"Helm, come starboard five points and up a shade," he ordered. "Bring Battery One into a better position to engage. Railgun teams, time to earn your kibble."

Laughter from his people.

Two missiles, at the shorter edge of range. Normally, you fired them from out a long ways, so that they had already separated and you had to deal with multiple fragments. Right now, the batteries could try to hit as they were still accelerating from a dead stop.

Helped when the shot was coming right at you, as the deflection fell to zero quickly.

Battery Three got a lucky hit almost immediately, then turned right back onto their target gunboat.

"Battery Four, I have a cooling system malfunction. Do we continue to engage?"

"Affirmative," Maddox replied instantly. "Burn them out if you have to."

He was staring at Padraig as he spoke. Padraig nodded.

Exactly correct logic. They could repair the turret and the cannon once they got back to Albany where they were safer.

"Battery Two, what is your status?" Maddox asked.

"Coming to bear now, sir."

Padraig watched a new targeting reticle appear on the gunboat. Two little gunboats against *Marrakesh* was as unfair as a Leviathan force against him.

"Missile two killed," came the call from the aft railgun team. "Anybody up there bothering to shoot bad guys?"

Padraig laughed out loud. Railgun pulsar teams often had nothing to do until those moments of pure panic as missile fragments got to terminal velocity and tracked. They tended to get teased in order of bore size by the other weapons teams.

They would always take the opportunity to dish it back.

"Aft turret, I have lock."

Padraig watched as the big gun suddenly spoke. First shot missed the stern of a suddenly frantically maneuvering gunboat. The second one spiked it just like that catfish.

Something exploded aft, wreathing the stern in a plasma cloud like a pink ballet tutu.

When it cleared, the front half of the gunboat was tumbling on all three axes of motion.

"Captain, the remaining enemy vessel has fled," Nyssa yelled loud enough to cause all voices to still.

The silence was almost palpable, like the blue fog around them had been for the last two days.

"Nothing left?" Padraig asked, a bit dumbfounded.

Had he just won and held the field of battle?

Against a LEVIATHAN?

"Affirmative, sir," Nyssa nodded.

He blinked, then his training kicked in.

"Scan for lifesuits from the two gunboats," he ordered. "Find me survivors that need rescuing."

"Sir?"

"Ships like that come apart pretty easily, Squire," Padraig reminded her. "The crews are trained to abandon ship as fast as they can when they lose hull integrity. Someone might be floating in space right now. It's a terrible way to die, all alone when your life support gives out."

"Understood, sir," she said.

Padraig dialed a number on his comm.

"Flight Deck. Rafferty."

"Air Boss, recall *Flight of Fancy*," Padraig ordered. "And get medical teams ready to deploy on *Roadrunner* once Nyssa gets you coordinates."

"Rescue operations, sir?" Walter asked.

"You got it."

"Do we need to include security forces?"

"Negative, Air Boss," Padraig replied. "We are rescuing marooned sailors. I doubt that anybody will be a problem child at this point."

"Understood, sir."

Padraig cut the line and leaned back. He sucked in a deep, cleansing breath and held it for a four count, releasing it all in a single blow.

Then he looked around at expectant faces.

Captain Boru smiled.

"Radio, track that Leviathan and let me know if they turn back for a second run while we're rescuing their people," he said. "Weapons, stand down at present, but keep the teams hot, just in case. Let Battery Four come offline so they can fix whatever broke. Helm, bring us around to a spot close to center on the two destroyed gunboats so our people have the shortest flight time."

He paused to give the words more weight.

"Oh, and people, good job," Padraig reminded them.

46

Padraig put on his best Captain's Scowl and went aft.

They'd managed to rescue three people from the two boats, which was two more than he'd honestly been expecting, with the way those vessels had ruptured. Medical had them for now, then they'd be put into isolation from his other problems until he could get back to Albany and off-load everything to someone else.

He was just a starship captain, not a spymaster.

Still, he had one last problem child to deal with, at least for now.

Cameron Farrell was standing her watch outside of a cabin. Chance had command from the bridge. Dr. Borsheva was standing next to Farrell, weight awkwardly shifting back and forth as she studied his approaching face.

"Status of the prisoner?" Padraig asked Cameron, ignoring Borsheva for now.

"Black eye from where Den tripped him into a bulkhead," Cameron replied. "Manacled to a stanchion with enough space to make it to the head. Meals delivered on a regular schedule and he just ate an hour ago. Left him with an entertainment tablet that has had the wireless connection broken physically. Generally a model prisoner once he woke up."

Padraig nodded. All the rest of Borsheva's people had been told that Dr. Donal had been arrested, but not why. Enough that they were not manacled, though the hatches were locked, with eight to a room. Crowded, but not stuffed in.

More humane, for the remaining time they were his problem.

Padraig turned to Borsheva.

Again, he was struck by a number of things about the woman. The skin a shade darker than his, almost down into bronze. Offset with the hair bleached chemically white, then tinted a strawberry blonde in a manner he might have expected of someone from *Wronlori*.

Impressively hard eyes, but he'd already known how brilliant the woman was.

"Anything you'd like to share before we go in there, Doctor?" he asked.

"I still can't understand it, Captain Boru," she shook her head. "He was always one of my best students. For him to turn like this makes no sense."

Padraig had his theories. Both Chance and Kaitlin had shared a few of their own.

He wanted it from the horse's mouth, as the ancient saying went.

Padraig turned to Cameron.

"Open it up," he ordered.

She went in first, but that was fine. There weren't many men on the ship as strong as Cameron Farrell. Kaitlin might have been, twenty years ago. Den Gilroy would be close. That was about it.

He felt safe with her leading.

The room was crowded. Ryan Donal remained on the bed and scowled angrily at everyone. Cameron loomed close enough to punch him in the other eye if he got pissy.

Padraig put Dr. Borsheva in the corner farthest away from the prisoner, then took the center of the compact room.

"We've found your radio," he said simply. "And a few other things that convince me you are a spy. Presumably for *Wronlori*, but that doesn't matter. I could order you executed based on the evidence I already have in hand."

He let that one slide, mostly to see the blink of shock course through the man's system.

Technically, Padraig would be in his power to do so. A dumb-ass move on his part, but he wasn't about to say that to the man.

Donal hadn't denied anything. Nor acted with any great innocence. Hopefully, they could jettison the charade of a terrible misunderstanding.

Padraig would not, however, rate the man as anything approaching a professional spy.

"Do you have anything to say that might mitigate things?" Padraig asked.

Cameron stood there looking tough. Dr. Borsheva remained silent in the corner.

"Nothing for you," Donal finally said, his eyes flickering over Padraig's shoulder.

"To Dr. Borsheva, then?" Padraig asked.

He watched a glare of pure murder link the two boffins.

Padraig had often wondered about the phrase *staring daggers at someone*, and now he understood what that actually meant.

"Why, Ryan?" Borsheva asked, pushing herself away from the wall to stand close to Padraig.

"Because I was never going to amount to anything with you in my way, Alexis," he snarled at his former boss.

"In the way?" she countered. "You were on your way to your own team, Ryan. Your own projects."

"Under your supervision, Dr. Borsheva," he growled back.

Cameron stirred, and Donal relaxed his sudden tension.

"You're the golden child, Alexis," Donal continued, in a weary voice like water drops landing on stone, slowly wearing it away. "You were always going to get the best budgets for research and development. I'd have had to be happy with the scraps."

"So, you wanted me killed?" she gasped.

"Removed," he sneered. "Captured by *Wronlori* and no longer a problem because we both know they'd have never traded you home. I'd have been in the same boat, but they were going to let me go to work for them. That was the deal. I'd get to invent a whole new generation of weapons, without having to listen to you explain that I was wrong about everything."

Padraig held his tongue. He remembered being young and full of crazy ideas about how the old farts didn't understand anything. How he could have changed the universe if only they'd put him in charge.

Thankfully, nobody had.

Today, he was that old fart with enough horizon to understand that most of his ideas wouldn't have worked. And the few that would have, he had already implemented on *Marrakesh*.

His officers would train future officers that way.

Tomorrow's issue, though.

Donal turned his head and locked eyes with Padraig now.

"I am a political prisoner and demand that you return me to *Wronlori*," the man said calmly. "I have asked for and been granted asylum and citizenship, so I am a prisoner of war."

"You are a spy," Padraig reminded him in a cold, hard voice. "Those three folks we rescued from the gunboats we destroyed were wearing uniforms of a recognized military and operating according to generally understood rules of engagement. You were not, Donal. Command gets to deal with you when we get home. Any other statements I should hear and ignore?"

The scowl was back. And his teeth were grinding, if that was the sound Padraig heard. Donal gave the most minute shake of his head.

"Very well," Padraig nodded. "You will remain my prisoner until I turn you over to the authorities at Albany. If you change your mind about talking, let me know."

He turned and gestured Dr. Borsheva out of the cabin, with Cameron following. She locked the hatch again and nodded.

"Standard watch rotation, Farrell," Padraig reiterated. "Nobody alone in there with him, even when meals are delivered. He'll be turned over to station security in a day or three and out of our hair."

"Understood, sir," she replied, planting her butt against the wall next to the door.

Padraig turned to Dr. Borsheva. She looked like she wanted to say something, but Cameron inhibited her.

"Shall we talk in my office, Doctor?" he asked.

That seemed to be what she needed.

He started forward.

47

Padraig got Alexis Borsheva settled in his office. Chance had joined them, taking the other seat, with Maddox in command on the bridge on the other side of the door.

Help was just six steps away, so Padraig wasn't worried. Everyone had risen above themselves this week and needed some rewards. And some downtime, but that was next week.

"I don't understand," Borsheva began when everyone got settled. "He had it all in front of him. Why would he throw it away like that?"

Padraig stirred, but Chance spoke first.

"Jealousy," she said.

"Of what?" Borsheva asked.

"Just about everything," Chance shrugged. "I talked to Kaitlin, and one word kept coming up when she described him. Average."

"Ryan Donal is one of the smartest people I have ever met," Borsheva countered.

"Compared to you, how smart is he?" Padraig asked.

Borsheva squirmed a little at that, so he figured she knew the truth.

"Not as smart," she said quietly, blushing badly enough that he could actually see the redness in her dark skin. "But that shouldn't matter!"

"A man's ego is a different thing, Dr. Borsheva," Padraig replied.

"Average looks," Chance ticked her finger on the table. "Average height. Average build. Average kind of everything, so he never stood out in a group. And not as smart as you, Alexis. I could see that twisting him. I had a boyfriend like that once, before Robin. Nice enough guy, but a little too neurotic for me."

"What will happen to him?" Borsheva asked, turning back to look at Padraig.

"He's going into military detention," Padraig replied. "There are specific rules for spies we manage to capture. Isolation, then turned over to specialists. Once he's off my deck, I suspect he'll disappear forever."

"Would they trade him?" she asked.

Padraig shrugged. None of it was his problem.

"I'm more concerned with the rest of your team, Dr. Borsheva," he countered. "How will they react to being functionally arrested?"

"Some of them will likely quit," she nodded. "Given their existing security clearances, I expect that everyone will have to go through a whole extra set of reviews, like they did before. The annual ones obviously were insufficient, if they missed Ryan's activities. Some will understand and return to work, but I suspect that this has cost me a year of development work."

"Can you go purely theoretical in that time?" Chance spoke up.

"What do you mean?" Borsheva turned back to his First Officer.

"Donal believes strongly that his theories represent some immense breakthrough, once he sorts out the math," Chance said. "Kaitlin mentioned some of her conversations with the man."

"Okay?" Borsheva nodded. "I am familiar with those ideas."

"And if you lose a lot of your team for a year, should you set out to prove Donal right or wrong?" Chance asked. "The math and physics don't necessarily need people besides you. And if they did trade him to *Wronlori*, it would be nice to not let him give them any sort of advantage, however small."

"Oh!" Borsheva chirped. "Yes, I see. That's a lovely idea, Chance. I'll start immediately."

Padraig started to say something, but the woman exploded out of her chair, hugged Chance, and fled in a flurry of knees and elbows, leaving him alone with his First Officer.

"That was interesting," he remarked dryly.

"She's really that smart, Padraig," Chance nodded. "Emotionally a little stunted, because every man or woman she's ever met isn't as smart as her. Most of them flee pretty quick."

"I see," he offered.

"We had several hours to just chat while sitting watch in that fog bank," Chance grinned. "Two girls, letting their hair down, metaphorically. Bex Magorian got in on it as well. It almost felt like a kid's sleepover at times, but for the guns part."

He nodded.

"Was there ever a moment between her and Donal?" he asked.

Chance paused, obviously reviewing conversations in a new light.

"No, but they might have gotten there at some point," Chance said. "She's his faculty advisor and mentor from school, so they couldn't really do anything like that until he was her peer. Maybe if he'd been a little less antsy to get wherever he was going, he might have seen that. Water under the bridge now."

"Agreed," Padraig nodded. "Water under the bridge. We'll see their backs soon enough and get on with whatever Command has for us. I'd like a quiet sail next time, in spite of the war."

They lapsed into silence. Chance had a question in her eyes, but wasn't ready to ask, so he waited.

The relationship between Captain and First Officer was, in many ways, at least as close as married spouses.

Chance had Robin, and Padraig didn't particularly find women attractive, so there was little risk there. At the same time, you did develop an emotional intimacy that was difficult for outsiders to understand.

That pairing usually set the stage for the rest of the crew. Fortunately, he had Chance Messier. Several years as a new mom, flying a desk at Headquarters, and finally ready to get back out and tackle deep space.

Padraig didn't have anyone at home. Not after Jean-Michele had decided that he didn't like the long separations that came with military service.

She drew a breath but didn't speak. Surged and receded.

"Ask, Chance," Padraig ordered in a light tone. "That's the only way to learn. And we should always be learning."

"That Leviathan," she finally said. "How did we defeat it? How did you do it?"

"I didn't do it, Chance," he corrected her. "You were right the first time. We did."

"Okay, how did we do it?"

"I had a plan," he admitted. "And I'm captain, so I'll get most of the credit, except where you and Kaitlin helped neutralize and capture an enemy agent."

She started to speak before he overrode her.

"Yes, you did," he said. "You got Borsheva to help. You and Kaitlin did the things. I just agreed, so if they pin medals on both of you, I'll be standing in the front row cheering with Den and Bex. You earned that part."

"And the rest?" she asked.

Her skin wasn't as brown as Borsheva's, so the blush was a little more obvious this time.

"I have good people," he replied flatly, including her by his tone. "We had to run and stay ahead of them so they didn't blast us out of Ghost-space. That's Zarah on the Helm and Jareth back on the machines. Nyssa found me the nebula to hide in, then got everything quiet, while still mildly jamming radio frequencies so that Donal's gizmo might not have worked."

"The thing he had originally built didn't have enough power to get it through the hull," Chance spoke up. "That was why he went back for more gear. He wanted to build some sort of amplifier."

"There you go," Padraig nodded. "A good team. Maddox figured out how to reprogram a missile. The Leviathan didn't fall for it, but it did unmask one of their gunboats."

"Yeah," Chance brightened up. "Why didn't we run when we knew that they either chased us without those ships, or had to stay behind?"

"Between you and me?" he asked. She nodded carefully.

"Son of a bitch pissed me off and I wanted a chance to serve them up a little revenge myself."

Her eyes got big, but she'd been flying a desk when Eworn first got that surprise attack. He'd been serving as First Officer aboard *Nemesis* that day, after a stint as Weapons Officer previously.

"Then, you and Dr. Borsheva—Alexis—calculated where to find a Leviathan for me," he continued. "At that point, we swarmed one of his gunboats with a Nine and got lucky. Then we got lucky again putting part of a Six into the mothership, after Den and his crew scored a direct hit to their A-turret and apparently hit an ammunition store from the way it vented and blew out power lines. Looking at Nyssa's logs, they lost a lot of forward firepower and their rear turrets were too ambitious covering forward arcs, so we got a hit home aft. Again, lucky, but I'll take it."

"Lucky," she repeated quietly.

"The old sailor's mantra, Chance," he nodded. "I'd always rather be lucky than good. You can be the best there is, but when the other guy gets lucky…"

He let that trail off.

Most battles were a matter of the luck running your way.

Or not.

He'd gotten lucky. *Marrakesh* had.

And he'd had the kind of crew that could take advantage of that luck.

They'd forced a Leviathan to flee from battle, killing two gunboats while badly damaging the ship itself.

"So now what?" she asked.

"Now, we declare those new guns a success and the fleet starts building them for refits and new hulls," Padraig nodded. "We swap out mission modules for the next thing that

Command has for us. I'd like something quiet, myself, but this is war, and the other guy exists to mess up your plans. That's why he's the enemy, after all."

"We'll handle it," she said, smiling and rising. "I need to get back to flying the ship."

He nodded her out.

They'd handle it.

Whatever the fates threw at them.

48

MEDICAL BAY, SUNDERING WRATH

Divna looked up from her reports when the hatch opened. She'd originally asked to be put in the general bay with the other sailors, but both Maric and the ship's Surgeon had refused and instead put her in a private room.

Maric entered now, with the tiny doctor trailing him, the woman plucking at his sleeve.

"She cannot be bothered for long," the surgeon implored him.

"I understand, Doctor," Maric nodded.

Then they were alone.

She was sitting up. In the process of gluing her scalp back together, they had shaved part of it. She'd had them remove the rest so she didn't look like some strange, teenage rebel.

That had been nearly forty years ago, after all.

She ran a hand over her smooth skin, carefully touching the healing scar that hopefully would vanish once she added bangs in another year.

Maric pulled a chair close and sat.

"How are you doing?" he asked in a quiet voice.

"Bored out of my mind," Divna replied with a wry grin. "But your doctor refuses to budge on allowing me to do anything for another twenty-nine hours and seventeen minutes."

He grinned back.

"She does take her job seriously," he offered. "Even I have been on the wrong side of that expert opinion a time or two."

Divna nodded.

Marshals were flag officers. In COMMAND. Until a medical professional certified them unfit for duty and confined her to a bed in a room with nobody else to talk to.

Even common sailors would have gotten over their hesitation, with everyone together. She'd have had *someone* to talk to.

"How is your ship?" Divna asked.

She had been assigned here for this mission. It was still his crew. His vessel.

They would share the failure equally, though Divna believed that most of the fault was hers.

"Some of the damage can be repaired in flight," Maric replied. "The forward turret may need a full drydock, after the explosion welded some pieces and blew out some bulkheads. Given that getting home was more important, we have not dropped into real space to deploy EVA crews in order to assess things. The shipyard will have to handle it."

Divna nodded. She'd suspected as much from the way the hull had trembled.

No memories after that, so she'd had to review bridge camera footage to see the flex that slammed her face first into the edge of the console too fast to even react.

No permanent damage, which was enough for now.

The same could be said of *Sundering Wrath*.

"The gunboats?" Divna asked.

"*Marrakesh* killed two of them," he grimaced. "One escaped and made it to rendezvous, plus the one that was damaged in cradle and unable to deploy."

"Your people paid a terrible toll," Divna said. "How are they holding up?"

"Angry," he nodded. "Embarrassed, I think is more accurate, but of course none will speak such things aloud."

Divna nodded. She felt the same way.

"Captain Boru is more than he seems," she said carefully.

"Sir?"

"What we knew of the man before did not suggest that level of skill," Divna continued. "I have been updating my personal logs with speculation but will not add such flights of fancy to the official record, lest we taint the next captain that has to deal with *Marrakesh*."

"It will not be us," Maric replied, eyes downcast.

"I would not be so sure, Captain," Divna corrected him.

His eyes came up, and she saw hope mingled with rage.

"Sir?"

"As I noted. *Marrakesh* should not have been able to do that," she replied. "That suggests that Captain Boru is far more dangerous than we presumed from him commanding a mere tug. Even a cruiser-scale one."

Maric waited, holding his breath.

"When we return to base, I intend to make a case to my own superiors that *Sundering Wrath* be allowed to hunt *Marrakesh* again, Captain," Divna pronounced. "They may allow it, once I share my unofficial notes with a Division or Fleet Marshal. It will take time to locate *Marrakesh* again, but *Sundering Wrath* will need that time to be repaired and have a new wolfpack trained. Would your crew be in favor of such a mission?"

"Moreso than just about any other thing they might send us after, Marshal Babic."

Divna nodded.

"I can make no promises," she said carefully. "So do not share this with your crew until I know more, but I plan to call in some favors and promises when we get home. I intend to destroy Captain Boru, once and for all."

Maric held out his hand and she took it.

"I will serve, however you need," he said.

"We will see it done, Captain," Divna said.

Inside her, the rage for vengeance burned.

READ MORE

Be sure to read the rest of the Operation Marrakesh series!

https://www.knottedroadpress.com/product-category/science-fiction/operation-marrakesh

ABOUT THE AUTHOR

Blaze Ward writes science fiction in the Alexandria Station universe (Jessica Keller, The Science Officer, The Story Road, etc.) as well as several other science fiction universes, such as Star Dragon, the Dominion, and more. He also writes odd bits of high fantasy with swords and orcs. In addition, he is the Editor and Publisher of *Boundary Shock Quarterly Magazine.* You can find out more at his website www.blazeward.com, as well as Facebook, Goodreads, and other places.

Blaze's works are available as ebooks, paper, and audio, and can be found at a variety of online vendors. His newsletter comes out regularly, and you can also follow his blog on his website. He really enjoys interacting with fans, and looks forward to any and all questions—even ones about his books!

Never miss a release!
If you'd like to be notified of new releases, sign up for my newsletter.

http://www.blazeward.com/newsletter/

Buy More!
Did you know that you can buy directly from the KRP website?

ABOUT KNOTTED ROAD PRESS

Knotted Road Press publishes dynamic fiction set in exotic locations and unique non-fiction voices in genres such as auto-biography, business, cookbooks, and how-to. Our authors cover a wide range of genres including science fiction, fantasy, mystery, literary, and poetry, appealing to all readers. We offer both DRM-free ebooks and print books for a global readership.

Knotted Road Press
www.KnottedRoadPress.com
www.KnottedRoadPress.com/Shop